The Wedding Favour

Michele Gorman writing as

Lilly Bartlett

OneMoreChapter

One More Chapter
a division of HarperCollins*Publishers*
The News Building
1 London Bridge Street
London SE1 9GF

www.harpercollins.co.uk

This paperback edition 2020

First published in Great Britain in ebook format by
HarperCollins*Publishers* 2020

A catalogue record for this book
is available from the British Library

ISBN: 9780008319687

This novel is entirely a work of fiction.
The names, characters and incidents portrayed in it are
the work of the author's imagination. Any resemblance
to actual persons, living or dead, events or localities is
entirely coincidental.

Set in Birka by Palimpsest Book Production Ltd, Falkirk
Stirlingshire

An enormous Thank You to Beth Thomas for helping me understand the process that the Home Office requires when seeking to marry a foreign national. Your expertise was invaluable!

Prologue

'Are you *positive* she's not dead?' My niece's worried whisper is so close to my face that I catch a whiff of her sweet Frosties-breath. At six, she's the perfect height to scooch onto the sofa where I've spent the night. The middle cushion has slid partway off, and no wonder, with its silvery brocade that always gave my clothes a fierce case of static cling when I perched there in happier days. My arse is wedged into the sofa's murky depths, definitely touching whatever is underneath, but I'm not about to move a muscle now.

'She's not,' Leo answers with his usual big brother authority. 'Mum says she only wishes she was. She's had a *hard time* so she's sleeping.'

He whispers the words, as if I've got a terminal diagnosis. He's not far off.

'But it's almost lunchtime.' Little fingers poke at my shoulder.

'Caitlin, don't. Mum said to leave her.' I can hear the start of a wrestling match as Leo subdues his sister.

I pry open one eye just in time to catch him snatching the biscuits Rowan left last night with my undrunk tea. 'Leave me alone, rug rats, and put those back! Can't a person have a mental breakdown in peace?'

Then I hear a ping. Finally! Better late than never. 'That's my phone!' Frantically, I fling things from the coffee table: balled up tissues, my bra, more open packs of biscuits than you'd find at a blood donation clinic. 'Where is it?!'

That sends them scattering. I must sound completely unhinged.

That's because I am completely unhinged.

'You're up,' Rowan calls from the lounge doorway. She doesn't wait for an invite to come into what is, technically, at this moment, my bedroom. She simply makes her way towards me, picking her way past my overnight bag (or rather *overnights*, plural), discarded clothes and seemingly every toy in the house. Still, she manages to get a march on. My sister-in-law never lets any stumbling blocks, literal or otherwise, get in her way.

Everything about Rowan screams efficiency, from the top of her no-nonsense (but still very cute) pixie cut to her always-in-ballet-flats feet. Pretty Ballerinas too, not knock-offs, on account of her high-flying programming job for one of the big banks. I had hoped my niece and nephew would inherit her looks instead of my brother's, but they've been cursed, like Paul and me, with the long Fraser nose, close-set eyes and furry brows that I have to pay good money at the salon to keep under control. Paul really should too, instead of walking around with a sleeping chinchilla on his brow. They did get our good lips, though, so that's something, and Rowan's pale blonde waves – though both Caitlin and Leo wear those longer than Rowan does – and they don't turn beetroot in five minutes of sun like their mum.

I'd take Rowan's lack of melatonin any day to get the rest of it. Imagine, if you will, the woman who really does have it all (without being smug about it like I'd probably be) . . . Well, that's Rowan. To this day I don't know how my brother ever convinced a gem like her to give him the time of day, let alone *marry* him.

But then, people are probably about to say the exact same thing about me and Matt.

'My phone, where is it?' How many times do I have to repeat myself before the importance of this question is impressed upon my family?

'I don't hear anything,' Rowan says. She tips her head like a spaniel listening for the tin opener.

'Not now. Before.' I reach under the sofa in case it fell from my heartbroken hand when I finally drifted off into fitful sleep.

'Oh, that. That was just the microwave. I'm heating up leftovers. Pizza. Mmm mmm. Want some? Oh, duck,' she says, catching my sob face, 'you don't have to eat it.'

She sits beside me. Credit to her, she only reels back a little bit when I slump into her arms. Must shower one of these days. 'I don't want pizza,' I snivel. 'I'd never eat pizza again if I could have Matt back.' Not that one has anything to do with the other. Or that I'd be able to keep the promise anyway. Blame my sorry state for making me resort to nonsense like this.

'Here's your phone.' Caitlin unplugs it from the wall. That's right. I'd wanted it charged in case his make-up call took more than 27% of my battery.

Now I'm fully charged but still broken up.

'Nobody rang,' she says, handing it to me.

'You're too young to be looking at phones,' I snap. Which is also ridiculous considering that she could practically build her own apps before she was out of nappies.

I feel like a first-class arse when Rowan gathers her daughter in for a hug. 'I'm sorry, love,' I tell Caitlin. 'I haven't been myself lately.'

'I know, Auntie Nelly, but there are other fish in the sea.'

'You didn't really just say that.'

Caitlin shrugs. 'It's true, isn't it?'

'I'll take dating advice from you when the Tooth Fairy no longer has to visit, okay?'

She sticks her tongue in the hole where her bottom tooth had been. 'I'm just saying what Mummy said.'

'Way to belittle my breakdown, Rowan.'

Now it's Rowan's turn to cast evils at her daughter. 'You're not having a breakdown. This is a temporary situation.'

'You mean you think we'll get back together?' I hear the desperation in my voice.

Rowan's eyes slide from mine. 'Maybe.'

'You're a hopeless liar.'

'I mean it might not be the worst thing if you didn't,' she says. She starts to gather up my tissue mountain but changes her mind. Instead, she folds over the ends of the biscuit packets. 'To be honest, he didn't always seem totally committed. He stayed away for Christmas.'

The cushion slides further towards the floor when I sit up. 'He got *food poisoning*, Rowan. You're not suggesting he purposely ate bad chicken to get out of seeing Gran. Trust me, he's totally committed. I mean, until we broke up. But I can fix this.'

Rowan shakes her head. 'I'm not sure you should, though, duck. You shouldn't have to convince a bloke to be with you.'

'Well, you would say that, wouldn't you, when my sap of a brother made it so easy. Meet, fall in love, get married, job done.'

Rowan, being Rowan, doesn't take it personally that I'm being a complete cow. She knows I couldn't have loved her more if she were my own blood sister. Luckily, she remembers it even when I talk like this.

'I'm saying that you're worth more, Nelly, that's all. And you know it. If someone hasn't got the brains to see that, then that's his loss, not yours. He hasn't bothered to ring you, has he?'

'It's only been three days.'

'And how many days is okay before he's an arse for not ringing his fiancée?'

'Ex-fiancée, apparently.'

'Just— Don't ring him, okay?'

'Okay.'

'Really okay? Or are you just saying okay until I leave the room and then you'll ring him?'

'Really okay.' I do have *some* pride left. Rationally, I know Rowan is right. I just need my heart to catch up with my head. And for Matt to ring me to apologise.

I can't bear to think about what it will mean if he doesn't.

I suppose I should come clean now, because you'll realise it sooner or later anyway. I'm the family screw-up. Not jailbird level. Just as in nobody is surprised when something else doesn't work out for me. There's always that knowing eye-roll. Like it's all my fault and what do you expect, *it's Nelly*.

But this *is* jailbird level. I'm the one about to be jilted. Never mind that my heart feels like it has been ripped in two. Oh, how everyone will pick over that with their Christmas dinner. Nelly's fiancé ran a mile rather than marry her.

Maybe I'll fake food poisoning this year.

PART ONE

FOR BETTER OR WORSE

Chapter 1

I haven't told anyone about me and Matt. And it's been nearly three weeks now. That makes me either the world's biggest optimist or completely delusional.

The problem is, the details of our last conversation are getting a little fuzzy. They say our minds do that when there's been a traumatic event, but you'd think something like this would be cemented into my memory, given that it's ruining my life. It's fair to say that I wasn't as coherent as I'd have liked, what with all the crying. I think I offered all kinds of promises when he started talking about taking a break.

A break. That's one word away from a break-*up*, but that's what he's done. He's gone on a break. Which is possibly why he hasn't returned my calls.

Rowan knows about us, obviously, since I wallowed all over her sofa for more than a week, but she's sworn to secrecy, and my brother's been out of town on one of his consultancy assignments (Abu Dhabi this time), so there's a chance it won't get back to the family yet. There haven't been any major events to cover for lately. Mum sometimes asks how Matt is when we talk, and I say 'fine' like I always have.

I suppose it's too much to hope that I can keep this up, that they won't notice the absence of a groom on the day itself.

I wish I had the stomach for it, but I cannot face everyone. Because it wasn't me who called time, was it? I'm the one everyone is going to wonder about. No matter how I spin it, I'm the jiltee, the rejectee, the un-fiancéed.

They're going to think I'm the defective one. Again.

I do remember that Matt was frustratingly vague about this whole break thing. That means there might still be a chance that we can make things okay. He's got to come to his senses at *some* point. I will not believe that this is the end. We were too good together to just throw away the best two years of our lives. Anyone would get cold feet with all the wedding planning we've been doing. I probably *have* gone a bit overboard on it all. Naturally, I offered to pare everything down to the bare minimum, if that's what he wanted. Even though we did decide on all the details together, and I'm not just saying that. Matt has made as many suggestions as I have, and we've agreed on them all. That's what I mean: nobody is as well-aligned as we are. So why hasn't he been in touch to admit he made a mistake?

It's the silence that's killing me. If we'd just broken up like normal people, then I'd get on with the usual stages of break-up grief. The share prices in Kleenex and Gordon's would go up. I'd baffle friends and strangers with unanswerable questions, maybe do something ill-advised with my hair. At least I'd be tragically thin, even if losing that ten pounds for the wedding dress would be a moot point.

I hate this limbo. Are we getting married in three months or not? I need to know. My family needs to know.

The country's biggest magazine *definitely* needs to know.

I should probably mention that too. The whole wedding is being paid for by *Fantastic Magazine*. All we have to do is let them cover the whole thing for the serialised wedding feature they're running.

If only that feature contest hadn't been so tempting, so perfect for us. Who wouldn't want to be chosen as the most romantic couple of the year, win ten thousand quid and get an entire series written about them?

I'll tell you the answer: a dumped fiancée, as it happens.

Sighing, I open the email again on my phone.

From: Martha@FantasticMagazine.co.uk
To: Nelly@FindingHappy.co.uk
Re: Release forms and prelim schedule

Dear Nelly,

Just a quick one to say again how excited we are to start the series. It's going to be a total inspiration for Fantastic Magazine's readers! Attached please find the release forms. An electronic signature is fine and we'll need them from everyone who'll be involved in the interviews and the photographing/filming. No rush to get them back. Here's a rough outline of what we'd like to photograph and interview about, but please do let me know if you have additional ideas – this is very much a collaborative effort, and it's your wedding after all! Like you said in your pitch, the more loved-up couple-i-ness the better, and the candid 'outtake' filming is such a great idea for the website! I'm sure we'll have more than enough for all three months' stories.

☐ *your falling-in-love story*

☐ *the dress (you said your mum will be there – anyone else?)*

☐ *decorations – will your friends/family help at all? That would make a great story*

☐ *flowers*

☐ *cake*

Other ideas:

☐ *wine tasting?*

☐ *will you do dance lessons?*

☐ *maybe bridesmaid's dresses? It might be interesting if they're different sizes and shapes*

We'll plan to be at your flat on the 27th. Is 10am too early?

See you sooooon!

Martha x

As if it's not bad enough that my fiancé might actually be calling off our wedding, I've got this to worry about. What am I supposed to do when Martha and her team turn up, expecting to follow us around for the next three months? Pretend Matt's in the loo the whole time?

This seemed like such an amazing opportunity, right when I'd been planning an entire life change. But I can't even *face* thinking about *that* right now.

It's not that I'm overly loyal to Martha, although I would feel terrible pulling out now. It's that I've also already spent the advance money for the feature on deposits for the wedding. I can't pay them back if I cancel the series.

Which means I also can't wait around for Matt to make up his mind.

I don't expect him to answer. I tap his name on my mobile again, trying not to be embarrassed by how many times it's said I've already rung.

'Hi, Nelly.'

'You answered! I mean, how are you?' My mouth has gone dry.

'Okay. Still trying to figure things out,' he says. 'That's why I haven't rung back. I did say I needed space.'

I can hear people in the background. Obviously he doesn't need space from everyone. 'Who's that?'

'Just some people I've met here.'

'Here? Where are you?'

He hesitates. 'Tarifa.'

Tarifa? As in Tarifa, *Spain*? 'You're on holiday while I'm worrying myself sick about our relationship?'

'It's not like that, Nelly,' he says. 'I told you I needed time to think. I had to get away from London. Everything reminds me of us. I took a sabbatical to sort my head out.'

'While you're on a beach.'

'It doesn't matter where I am. And it's not a holiday. I'm in an apartment.'

'You've *moved* there?' How has this happened? One minute we're making our guest list and the next he's making Spanish omelettes in his new apartment.

'Nelly, relax, of course I haven't moved. It's just that an apartment is cheaper than a hotel. I'm not having fun here, you know. I'm trying to figure things out.'

'If that was true, you could have gone to . . . I don't know, somewhere that doesn't have twenty-four-hour sangria and wall-to-wall bikinis. Who are you figuring things out with anyway?'

'No one! Nelly, this isn't about anyone else. It's about me. Us. Besides, I'd never do that to you.'

'But you would leave me three months before our wedding.'

'I haven't left you.'

'Matt, you're in a different time zone. What's your definition of leaving? Can you blame me for being worried? I don't even know if you *love* me anymore.'

'Of course I do. That's not the issue.'

'What's the issue, then? Because I'm more than a little confused. The last time I checked, we were in love and about to get married. Now you're partying it up on a windsurfer.' That Kleenex and Gordon's binge is fast looming on the horizon. 'The magazine is coming on the twenty-seventh. Exactly *what* am I supposed to tell them?'

'I don't give a damn about the magazine, Nelly, though clearly that's still uppermost in your mind.'

I'm so sick of this argument. It's not my fault that Matt doesn't get the whole social-media thing, or that I'm trying to build a career out of it. He thinks I'm Instagramming pouty selfies and photos of my breakfast. He can't see that this is how I'm finally going to make a success of myself.

You see, I've got this blog. So far, so shallow, but hear me out.

It started as somewhere to dump all my thoughts. Hardly anyone read it and that was fine with me. My friends were sick of hearing the same stories over and over. I *wanted* to offload into an anonymous void. It's what helped me be brutally honest about my life. About myself. And finally, instead of feeling awful, I actually started looking for ways to be happy.

Well, apparently I'm not the only one looking, because what started as a few people commenting on my posts has, four years later, turned into a community of thousands who read the blog every single day.

We gee each other up on Instagram. We're *there* for each other. And though we've never met in person, some feel like real friends – they *are* real friends, and I love them. They've been with me through all the ups and downs, and the ups again when I met Matt. They're looking forward to our wedding almost as much as I am. #superromantic!

It was easy to start posting on Instagram – and I admit that there was a bit of trout-mouth and breakfast-snapping in those early days – but once more people started engaging with the blog, my account really built up.

Then one day I got an email from a company. They wanted me to feature their inspirational tote bags! Well, things sort of took off from there.

With the magazine deal, the blog will get the exposure it needs to let me quit my day job and become a full-time *influencer*. I know, what a ludicrous word. Call it what you like, the point is that I can't earn a living as a blogger without a deal like this.

But if Matt breaks up with me, it won't only be my relationship that ends. My future career goes too. I can't give readers a break-up story. It's too depressing. 'Well, I'm sorry, but we made a commitment,' I tell Matt. 'You agreed, remember? While you're working on your tan, I'm trying to hold everything together here.' Then I get a terrible thought. 'Did you tell anyone? That you're backing out?'

'I'm not definitely backing out. Can't you give me some space?'

'Matt. Space is not seeing each other for a few nights so we can go home to do our laundry. Why can't you just admit that you're backing out? *Did* you tell anyone?' I know he didn't put anything on Facebook, because he's not on there. I guess I should be grateful for that, though it does make it impossible to see what he's doing every second of the day like I want to.

'Only my parents,' he says. 'I had to when I went away.'

That explains why I haven't heard from his mother. She usually checks in. Now she's avoiding me. 'Matt, help me understand what's wrong. Please.'

I can hear him take a sip of something. I bet it's alcoholic and frosty in the sunshine. It's overcast here. 'I keep thinking back to when we were first together,' he says. 'We were perfect for each other.'

I'm so tempted to answer him, to tell him I feel the exact same way. But I have to let him talk. I've asked the question. Now I need to hear the answer.

'And you know I wasn't looking for a relationship. It just sort of went that way. With everything being so nice and fun between us, it was easy. I'm just not sure it's really what I want.'

'But you asked me to marry you,' I point out. He definitely did. I might be fuzzy on more recent details, but I remember every second of that morning: the overcooked scrambled eggs in bed, just 'because', he'd claimed. The way he'd kept watching me while we ate, until I asked him what was wrong. How awkwardly he'd held my hand over the breakfast tray, dragging my sleeve through the buttered toast. And then his question, without preamble: will you marry me?

'I know,' he says now. 'That's because I do love you. I do. You've got to believe that. Even if I'm not sure about being married, I do love you. This really isn't about you. I hope you can believe me. I might not be ready for such a commitment. Not yet. But you've got everything planned already, and with the magazine coming . . . it makes it so official.'

Finally, an answer! I've been wracking my brains for weeks trying to figure out how to fix this, and finally I know. 'What if I cancelled the magazine? Would that help?' It won't help me, but sod it. My relationship is more important. I'll figure out how to pay Martha the advance back later. Maybe I can get a second job. The important thing is that I can fix this now.

'It might,' Matt says.

That doesn't sound completely fixed. 'Might? Or would?'

'I'm not sure,' he says.

'That's not enough for me.'

'No, I didn't think so. That's why I didn't ask you to do it.'

What am I supposed to do now? Give up the magazine and my chance to change my career along with it, in the hope that he'll eventually come around?

'This is why I need the time, Nelly,' he goes on. 'I've got to figure things out before we can go forward. I'm sorry. I know it's not ideal.'

'I can't wait around forever for you to decide what you want, Matt. I've got a week before I need to know. It's the twenty-seventh when the magazine gets here. At least give me the courtesy of telling me by then.'

This is just great. He's off at the beach and I'm stuck holding the wedding goodie bag. Or not, as the case may be.

Chapter 2

It turns out Matt doesn't need the whole week to decide our future because two days after our call, he emails me.

Email! The flippin' coward.

He understands, he says, if I want to go on with my life. What's that supposed to look like anyway?! Telling everyone I know that I've been jilted? Going to debtor's prison for not being able to pay back the magazine advance? Wallowing until I've cried so much that I actually die from dehydration? He says that since he can't make a decision in the time I've given him, he'll need to say no for now. Like I've offered him a second helping of peas, not my heart.

So that's it. I am officially a dumped woman. I'd love to say it's not as bad as I feared, but it's actually worse. My double-crossing mind keeps replaying our greatest hits to maximise my misery. Thanks, brain, for reminding me of all the times he turned up after work with a picnic so we could sit in the park on warm summer evenings or the way his face looked extra gorgeous when he was sleeping.

And I'm ever so grateful to have his proposal on loop, like some sick-making ride I can't get off.

As if things couldn't get any worse, I'm going to have to face my family next week at my dad's birthday party. They'll definitely ask where Matt is. What am I supposed to say, that he's got food poisoning again? They'll think I'm marrying someone with serious digestive issues . . . when, actually, I'm not marrying anyone at all, am I? #dumped.

Meanwhile, I've had to keep posting on my Instagram account every day as if nothing has happened. Believe me, that's not easy with all this crying. I've resorted to taking selfies with dark sunglasses on. It's only a matter of time before people start thinking I've had glaucoma surgery.

'How are you doing?' my co-worker Jenny asks as she stops by my desk. She's making a remarkably ugly sad face. Her eyes practically close as she scrunches up her expression, and I can see the remnants of a cold sore when she juts out her bottom lip. Normally she's the prettiest one here, so I'm touched that she puts herself out like this for me.

I've only told my office about me and Matt because they're a safe audience. Other than fearing that I'm going to blub all over them in the corridor, most of them have no skin in this game. I've been practising on all the non-essential people I can find – colleagues, one of my neighbours, the guy at the café around the corner who makes my tea just the way I like it. I'll work my way up to actual friends and, oh, God, my family.

'How long till I can go home?' We both look at the wall clock.

'I'm sneaking off early to meet a friend,' she says. 'Why don't you come? It'll be fun.'

With the way I'm feeling, she could have asked me to join her for a two-for-one smear test and it would've been infinitely preferable to sitting at my desk right now with thoughts of Matt running around my head. Besides, I don't want to be at work this week even more than I usually don't want to be at work.

I don't hate my job, per se. Like almost everyone who has to get up for the Monday morning commute, I just wish I didn't have to do it. But those insurance claim forms won't process themselves, will they? You can only aspire to imagine the glamour of my work week.

'Let's go,' I tell her, shoving my phone into my handbag.

I don't know who I expect Jenny's friend to be, but it isn't a six-foot-something Colombian who looks like he's on the national volleyball team. Once he's kissed Jenny's cheeks, Rafael flashes me the friendliest smile I've ever seen. 'Hi, nice to meet you,' he says, taking my hand. 'Please, let me get the next round in.'

'Wow, he's . . .' I say after he goes to the bar.

Jenny nods. 'I know. His accent makes me think of piña coladas.'

'Was that penis coladas? Did you and he ever . . .?' Supposedly she's got the perfect boyfriend, but I thought the same thing a month ago. One never knows.

'Nah, definitely not,' she says. 'He's friends with Ed, for one thing, and, actually, Rafael got me my job. He works upstairs in account management. Haven't you ever seen him in the building?'

'Uh-uh, not that I remember.' Though, staring at his broad back now, how could I have missed him? Love must have blinded me . . . No, stop that, Nelly. You will *not* think about Matt now, not when this is your first time out since The Email. Let's try to have one snot-free hour, shall we?

'You said for one thing,' I point out to Jenny. 'What's the other thing?'

'There's no other thing. He's gorgeous, isn't he? I can't, but you definitely should.'

This is a strange conversation to be having with a work friend, especially since, other than Jenny telling me that she has a boyfriend, we've never really talked about relationships before. Our social interaction hasn't progressed much beyond rubbishing colleagues who leave the milk out of the office fridge.

'You know that the best way to get over a bloke is to get under another.' Her smile is pure smut.

Rafael joins our laughter as he approaches the table. 'What are we talking about?'

'Home truths,' Jenny says. When I clink my gin and tonic with their drinks, Jenny catches my eye. 'Nelly is recently single,' she says.

I kick her under the table. Hard.

Rafael trains his deep brown eyes on mine. 'Recently? I'm sorry to hear that, if you're sad.'

We all stare at each other. 'Well, this isn't awkward at all,' I finally say.

'Sorry, I shouldn't have said anything.' Then Jenny turns to Rafael. 'Onto safer subjects, I hope. How's the visa hunt going?'

He shrugs. 'Nothing so far. There's no way to extend my work permit. They got a solicitor to look into it.' His sigh is monumental. 'I've got nine more months. Then . . .'

'But you can't leave when your whole life is here!' she says. 'That's not fair. You've been here, what, ten years?'

'Almost nine. I wish it was ten, then I could apply for settlement. It's not looking good.' He sips his pint. 'I don't like thinking about what will happen. My friends are all here, my career, my kids.'

'Oh, you've got kids?' I ask.

'Rafael is a football coach,' Jenny explains. 'Where is it? Hackney?'

'Yeah, Dalston,' Rafael says. 'And Kensal Rise. Of course they can replace me, but I'd hate to leave those kids.'

'Oh, you're only being modest,' says Jenny. 'You started the programme.' Then, to me she points out, 'He started it as an after-school thing to keep teenagers occupied and off the street. Didn't you win an award for that? He won an award and everything.'

Rafael looks embarrassed. 'It was very much a joint effort with the youth centres. Anyway, Immigration doesn't seem to value my local community award as much as you'd imagine.'

'Well, they should! You contribute to the country, plus you pay your taxes, which is more than a lot of foreign companies do. Not to mention that you always get your round in. Rafael, you're an asset to Britain.'

He laughs. 'I'll be sure to add that to my application. I probably wouldn't have minded so much five or six years ago, but Bogotá doesn't feel like my city anymore. I think of myself as a Londoner.'

'That would be hard,' I say, 'When you've spent so long in a place, made it home. I can't imagine having to leave the country.'

'Thanks, now I feel loads better,' he says. But he's smiling.

'And you definitely couldn't marry Mabs?' Jenny asks. Then she turns to me. 'That's Rafael's best friend.'

'Unfortunately not,' says Rafael. He looks so sad. 'She's on the same visa as me. If you hear of anyone, though . . .'

Wow, marrying for a visa. You hear about this kind of thing, but I've never actually met someone in that position. Though I suppose he's not the kind of person the *Daily Mail* likes to talk about. He's got a better job than me, and if he's starting up youth clubs and such then surely it's a benefit to have him here.

The plan starts forming in my mind before I've finished my drink. If Rafael needs someone to marry, and I've got a groom-shaped hole in my wedding plans anyway, then why couldn't we? It could – if I'm very smart about it –

solve both our problems. I wouldn't even have to pay the advance back to the magazine if I've still got a groom-to-be. And a very photogenic one at that. It's not like I'd be giving anything up with Matt to do it, now that the bastard has done a runner.

It's either the gin or the idea that's making my tummy fizz. Nobody *needs* to know that it's just a business transaction.

Who says that Matt was the one to call things off anyway? Except for Matt, admittedly. I can tell my side of the story whatever way I want, so why couldn't I have finally ended things with Matt after Rafael and I met a few months ago? A little back-dating won't hurt. It might even help his case with the Immigration people. We won't seem quite so whirlwind that way. Lots of people meet and marry within a year. My parents did.

It *would* mean that people would think I was a cheater, though. I guess I can live with the reputation, given that my other option is for everyone to think that I'm too sad to marry.

I know I can trust Rowan with my secret. Jenny might be a problem, though, if she knows I only met Rafael tonight. I'll have to think about that.

But would Rafael really do it? He might be all talk and no walk.

Well, you know what they say. Only one way to find out.

* * *

'How nice to hear from you,' he says when I ring the next day.

It was simple to find his office number, given that he works for our company. Luckily, there's only one Rafael in the account management department. Otherwise I might have been about to proposition a fifty-something bloke with chronic bad breath and a squint.

'You too. I mean—' Crikey, I'm nervous. 'I'm ringing because, well, this would probably be better in person, but I don't want to take up your time and, well, this is quicker. Like ordering a takeaway.' *Ordering a takeaway?*

'How can I help you, Nelly?'

'I could marry you,' I blurt. 'I mean, I'm British and single, so if you needed me to . . . to stay here, then I could. If you wanted.'

'Uh . . . you're right, that is a surprising phone call. I'd hate to see how you order a takeaway.'

'I don't offer marriage in exchange for a side of garlic bread, if that's what you mean. It's a straight business offer . . . unless you were joking about getting married.' Thank goodness this isn't a FaceTime call. He can't see my face burning.

'I didn't imagine becoming a mail-order groom,' he says, 'but it *would* solve my problem. You'd do this for me?'

'I'd do it for me, actually.' Then I tell him my situation. I mean the whole truth, without holding anything back. 'So, you see, it would be good for both of us. If it works.'

I can picture his smile as he laughs. 'I don't have much choice at this point. I'm pretty desperate.'

'Thanks. That'll make the perfect wedding vow on the day.'

'I'm sorry, I didn't mean . . . I'm sure you're a reasonable person to marry.'

'Stop spoiling me with all these compliments or my head won't fit through the door. Besides, recent events would suggest otherwise.'

'That was a pretty shitty thing for your ex to do,' he says. 'No matter what, you didn't deserve him to end things like that.'

'Thanks. The point is that we're in the same boat, for different reasons. I haven't got much choice, either, since I can't pay back the magazine advance. I've been working out a few details. There's lots more, obviously, but it seems like the big thing is how and when we met, since it would come as a surprise to everyone we know.'

'And how it would work practically too,' he says. 'It would look odd if we didn't live together after we're married, no?'

'I hadn't thought of that.' To be honest, there's a lot I probably haven't thought of. Walking up the aisle with Rafael is one thing, but how are we supposed to carry on after we've cut the wedding cake? 'Maybe it's a stupid idea.'

'Let's see if the details could work,' he says. 'I could meet you tonight if you're free. Nelly, you might be my saviour. Thank you for considering this. It would mean the world to me.'

'That's me, Saint Nelly. I can meet you any time from six-thirty.'

This is crazy. Absolutely crazy.

By the time I reach the pub where we're meeting, I'm actually starting to believe that this isn't the most off-the-wall idea in the world. Right? Right?! I mean, it's not as off-the-wall as contact-lens jewellery, two-person jumpers or entire Christmas dinners in a tin, and people actually buy those. This isn't as daft as sharing a jumper. This is . . . let's call it a creative solution.

So, I shouldn't really be this nervous when I catch sight of Rafael already waiting for me outside the pub. I hope his being even earlier than me means he's starting to believe in the idea too.

'Hi!' we both say at once. He leans down to kiss my cheek just as I lean up to kiss his. Unfortunately, he goes for the wrong cheek, which leaves us having to duck and dive to avoid a snog.

'Do Colombians go to the right?' I wonder as we make our way inside. Oh, God. That sounds like I'm asking about the way he adjusts his bits in his pants. 'Kisses, I mean.'

'I never really thought about it,' he says. We're both trying to look as if we haven't just nearly mashed lips. 'But I can't speak for my entire country. I'm right-handed, does that make a difference?'

He's smirking. I hope he's not thinking about his bits.

'It's just that it's left first, then right,' I say.

'I did kiss your left cheek first.'

'No, I mean you have to *go* left first. You kiss this side first.' I tap my right cheek. That just calls attention to the fact that I'm blushing. 'That's the way it's done.'

'Are you always this bossy?' he asks.

'Do *you* always kiss wrong?'

His smile is devastating as he slowly shakes his head. 'No complaints so far.'

I bet.

I've recovered some composure by the time we wedge ourselves into one of the corners. It's near the loos, but at least we're away from the main part of the busy pub. The rain lashing the windows is keeping everyone from spilling out onto the pavement like they probably usually do in nice weather. It's got that kind of drinking-on-the-pavement feel to it, with its rounded bar and dark wood trim, high panelled ceiling and hanging baskets outside.

'So, you want to marry me,' Rafael says, too loudly judging by the way one of the blokes beside us looks over.

Lowering my voice, I say, 'I feel like there's an opportunity to solve both our problems. If you were serious about it.'

'Serious as a heart attack,' he says. 'But what about you?' He sips his pint. 'Is this really worth it for you?'

'I don't have much choice,' I tell him, 'unless I want to pay all the money back. I mean, if I could pay it all back. Which I can't. So I'm stuck.'

He taps his pint to my glass. 'Then it's just what I've

always wanted. A woman who's got no choice but to marry me.'

'Talk about a fairy tale,' I answer. 'I've always dreamed of being married for my passport. We'll make a fine pair. If we can work out the details.' As I catch sight of us in one of the old-fashioned advertising mirrors on the wall, I think: we do look like a fine pair.

I wish I'd spent more time touching up my make-up.

'So how are we going to do this?' he asks. 'It's easy for me. Well, easier. My family are all in Colombia. I only need to let my parents know. They're more efficient than the postal system there. But you might have to deal with questions in person, no?'

'We might have to,' I correct. 'My parents will never go for this if they don't meet you first. Not that they need to give their permission. I just mean that they'll be suspicious.'

I haven't historically been known in my family for restraint when it comes to romance. I've practically asked new boyfriends to meet my parents before we've finished the first date. As it is, they're going to have a hard time believing that I've hidden Rafael for this long.

'I'm happy to meet your parents,' he says. 'Parents love me. And our friends? We'll have to tell them too.'

'It's a lot to sort out. Let's approach it logically. One step at a time.'

We both sip our drinks. Then we get down to the business of inventing the lie of our lives for everyone we know.

Chapter 3

Rafael and I are actually doing this! I sneak another peek at him as we speed on the train through the rolling hills and farms of Cornwall. He's sitting in the window seat, so I can pretend I'm interested in the view while I stare at him. He smiles when he catches me looking. Then he does the most remarkable thing. He envelops my hand in his.

'We should be practising, no?' he whispers. His voice sounds growly when it's low like this.

'Definitely. For authenticity.' That's the most important part of this whole crazy plan. Everything has to look completely real. One slip-up and the whole thing fails.

'I have an idea. Excuse me,' he says to the middle-aged woman sitting opposite. With a bit of squirming, he digs his phone from his pocket with his free hand. 'Could you possibly take our picture? I'm sorry to bother you but this is a big day. I'm about to meet my fiancée's parents.'

The woman makes an aw-bless face as she accepts both our phones. 'Smile!' she says, snapping away. She's still smiling when she goes back to whatever she's watching on her iPad.

Our heads nearly touch as we examine the results. 'Our first couple photos.'

'I've got one eye closed in that one,' I say.

'Authentic.'

By the time we met the other night (far from our office where there was no chance that we'd bump into Jenny), I was certain that I was off my trolley. But Rafael didn't seem to think so, and we figured out all the details that could scupper the plan.

I really hope we're not wrong, but we seem to have a water-tight story now. The most obvious question (and one that I get the feeling Immigration will ask) is: why haven't we got any emails, texts or phone calls till now if we got together months ago? Fair question, Your Honour, and the answer *is* a bit delicate. Since I was involved with my former fiancé when I met Rafael, naturally I didn't use my mobile. And I didn't really need to anyway, since I could just walk upstairs to his office. Which is, incidentally, how we met. Yes, it *is* very convenient, Your Honour. No, not very nice to my fiancé (former fiancé!), but you can't stop the heart wanting what the heart wants. I ended things with Matt when I knew I couldn't be happy with anyone but Rafael.

Hopefully, now, whenever I get weepy, I can blame it on the emotion of being newly in love instead of newly dumped.

Rafael is still holding my hand. 'Tell me something more

about your family.' He really does have the thickest black lashes I've seen outside of a Lancôme advert.

In the interest of a full briefing, I haven't held anything back from him. This is a straight business transaction, albeit with a walk up the aisle together at the end. It's quite liberating, this not having to pick and choose my words or worry what someone thinks of me.

We're all on our best behaviour in a new relationship, right? When it's real, I mean. Nobody wants to frighten the life out of a partner until they have to. Not that I'm comparing Rafael and Matt in any way, but it was months before I even mentioned my parents to Matt. They're definitely not a new-relationship topic.

Rafael is under the illusion that having all this foreknowledge will help, that he understands what he's walking into with my family. He doesn't. My parents have to be experienced to get the full picture.

'Well, Mum claims that Dad's deaf,' I tell him as the sea comes into view out the window. I love this bit, when we turn towards the north coast after travelling down the middle of Cornwall. 'But that's usually when he doesn't do what she asks. Sometimes he's stalling for time, till he can come up with an answer she'll accept. Mum's sharp, to the point of being prickly sometimes, but you'll get on well with my dad. He loves playing host.'

As long as he doesn't get too generous with his drinks. All bets are off with Dad once he's on a bender.

'Are you sure you don't want to warn them about me?'

'No way,' I say. 'I need the element of surprise on my side. Believe me, you don't know these people . . . Thanks for coming with me.'

It's Dad's birthday weekend. What better time to tell your parents that the wedding is still on, but that they'll need to spell the groom's name R-a-f-a-e-l on their cards.

'What are fiancés for?' He drops my hand but then flips up the arm rest between us and flings his arm over my shoulder. I could get used to this, despite always agreeing with Matt that public displays of affection are over-the-top yuck.

As we pull into St Ives station, I feel like my tummy is eating itself. If my parents don't believe us, then there isn't much point in carrying on with this charade. Mum would never go along with it for the magazine interviews, so I wouldn't even get out of paying back the advance. Which I can't do. My entire future is riding on the next few hours.

'This is stunning,' Rafael says. He's looking out over Porthminster beach. The gulls glow white above us in the deep blue sky. The sea is calm today. Mum said it's been dry here.

I aim my phone at the horizon. #beachtastic. My followers can't get enough of my Cornwall pics. 'Bogotá is a big city, right?' I ask him as I squint at my screen in the bright sunlight. 'Near the water?' I add a few more hashtags. 'Come here. We'll get one together.'

'Not even close,' he says. 'It's landlocked.' Then he smirks as I pull my selfie stick from my bag. 'Seriously?'

'It's very practical.' A man shoots me a dirty look as he hops away from the waving stick.

'Yeah, I can tell. Why not just ask someone to take a photo?'

'Because that's bothersome.'

'Much better to take out people's eyes.'

Ignoring him, I snap a dozen or so pictures.

'Why did you ever leave here?' he asks. When he closes his eyes to breathe in the warm breeze, I get a glimpse of what he'd look like asleep. He'd give Matt a run for his money in the gorgeousness department.

Stop thinking about Matt, I chide myself. It'll only start me crying again, and then Mum will never believe I'm happy and in love with Rafael. What's done is done. This is my life now.

'You're very lucky that your parents are here,' he adds.

'Wait till you meet them,' I warn, shoving Matt out of my head and my phone back into my bag.

It's a short walk from the station to the house, where we find Mum and Dad sitting in the back garden at the big old farm table that's been weathered to a shimmery silver. They practically live out here in nice weather. Mum's munching toast between sips of the no-doubt cold tea that she claims not to mind drinking. She says her job means she has to abandon her cuppa at the office whenever clients call. I think she just likes to be a martyr.

She and Dad have identical smiles to mine plastered on their faces as we approach. 'I've got a surprise,' I tell them, because there's no use hoping they don't notice that it's not Matt by my side. 'Mum, Dad, this is Rafael.'

Formally, he shakes my parents' hands. 'So nice to finally meet you,' he tells them both.

I can tell that Mum catches the *finally*.

'Nelly didn't mention . . . You're a friend of Nelly's?' Dad might look as jovial as Father Christmas (minus the snowy hair and beard), but don't be fooled. A shrewd man lies just beneath that chubby, red-faced surface. He might not be quite as quick as Mum (nobody is), but he almost always knows when I'm up to something.

Rafael and I reach for each other's hands. The warmth of his does make me feel a bit better. 'Like I said, I've got a surprise for you.' They must be able to hear my heart clacking. 'We're in love. I've broken up with Matt and now I'm marrying Rafael.'

My mother's mouth drops open. 'You're— You've— You're . . . what? What?'

'Yep,' I tell her. 'Rafael and I are getting married.' The only way I'm going to survive this is to brazen it out. If I keep talking, there's a chance I'll get through it. Mum's a solicitor. In other words, suspicious for a living. If I let her have any time to think, she'll only start picking holes in our story. 'I know it seems sudden, but it's not, really. We met months ago, at work, didn't we?' Here, Rafael's arms encircle me as he hugs me to him. 'I've never met anyone like him and the more we saw each other, at work, I mean, because we weren't dating, obviously, because I was with

Matt, the more I realised that I couldn't go on with the wedding plans, given the way I feel about Rafael. It wouldn't have been right, so I told Matt a few weeks ago.'

This blathering on is part of the plan, till they get over the initial shock.

Mum's delicate eyebrows scrunch together as she frowns. I didn't inherit those eyebrows. Or her pale bobbed hair or the kind of figure that makes women half her age jealous (speaking for myself). 'You're saying that Matt is out and Rafael is in?'

'That's what I'm saying. Everything else is the same: the date, the venue, the registry. And Paul is still standing up for Rafael.'

'Matt's sister is still your maid of honour?' Mum asks.

'Obviously not, Mum! It'll be Rafael's best friend, Mabs.'

'And Matt knows?'

'Oh, yes. He's gone off to Spain on sabbatical. Actually, we talked just last week.'

'That's very . . .' Dad trails off.

'Mature,' Mum finishes. 'But you've known each other . . . how long, you and Rafael?'

'Since the beginning of March, but we've seen each other every day at work. Not *seeing* seeing each other. Till I told Matt. Now we're seeing each other properly. At night.'

Now it's Dad's turn to frown. Why did I have to put that image into my father's head?

'That's not very long to know each other before getting married,' he says.

I'm ready for this. 'You and Mum were engaged in three months and we've known each other almost twice as long. We're just being practical, Dad, with everything already underway and all. Believe me, I didn't plan for this to happen.' That could not be truer.

My mother sits back down. 'Well, you're right, this is quite a surprise. I thought you were going to tell me you lost your job.'

Rafael's frown is almost imperceptible, but I catch it. He hugs me tighter. It's a little gesture, and I know we're in character right now, but I am so grateful for it.

'I'm gasping for a tea,' I say, instead of thanking Mum for her vote of confidence about my ability to support myself. 'Who wants another? Rafael can help me.'

Mum bounces to her feet. 'I'll do it. You're a guest, Rafael. You don't need to work. Nelly can help *me*.'

No way. She wants me alone for questioning. I'm invoking the Geneva Convention. I have the right to have a representative with me. Yet it's ludicrous for us all to go into the kitchen together. Like pouring water on teabags is a four-person job.

'Let me give you a hand, Mrs Fraser,' Rafael says. 'If I'm going to be in the family, then I need to learn how you like your tea, no?'

Wow, is he good or what? I watch them walk together towards the house. Rafael towers over my mum as he ambles beside her. 'Have you been to Cornwall before?' I hear her ask as they go into the kitchen through the open sliding door.

So far, so good.

'You want to tell me what's going on?' Dad says. He digs another Hobnob from the packet.

'Don't you want to wait for your tea?'

'I'll have another with my tea. Don't tell your mother. I had to buy this packet as it was.' He pats the swell of his tummy beneath his golf shirt. Dad hates golf, but he does love the uniform. His closet is full of them, neatly ironed in every colour. It's all he wears. Mum's going to have a hard time getting him into a suit for the wedding. 'What's really going on?' he asks.

'Nothing, Dad, honest. I know it's a lot to take in, but this has happened.' I shrug. 'I'm in love with Rafael.'

'Just like that. What about Matt?'

'Why are you suddenly so concerned about him? You never really liked him anyway.'

'We never got the chance to know him properly. We might have liked him if he'd bothered turning up at family dos.'

'*One* Christmas, and you both hold that against him. He had food poisoning!' Wait a second. Why am I defending Matt when he's probably rubbing sun cream into some sexy Spaniard as we speak? 'It doesn't matter now. You can get to know Rafael instead. He's amazing.'

My smile this time isn't an act. I couldn't have picked anyone better to pull this off with. He's as desperate for it to work as I am. Maybe more so. If it were to go wrong, I'd only lose face and my credit rating. Rafael would lose his whole life.

When he and Mum return with our teas, I find myself checking for any signs that she got to him: terrified eyes or maybe the telltale tap of 'help' in Morse code on his tea mug. But his smile is as relaxed as usual.

'So, Bob, Rafael has been telling me about Colombia,' Mum tells Dad, turning the handle towards him when she hands him his mug. Then she takes the Hobnob packet and tightly twists the top closed. I wait about three seconds before untwisting it. Then I fish one out and loyally offer the packet to Dad. 'That's where he was born, in Bogotá. Isn't that interesting?'

'But he's been here since after university,' I add. 'That was almost ten years ago.' The less they talk about his foreignness, the better. Mum's area of law isn't immigration (it's conveyance), but still.

'Oh? Dual passport, then?' Mum asks.

Danger, danger!

Rafael's answer is as smooth as her question. 'No, I've had a work permit through my company for many years. And you don't need to worry about me stealing Nelly away from here. The UK is my home. Now it will be our home together.'

Instead of sitting down in the chair closest to him, he drags it around the table to plonk it beside mine. His fingers gently stroke my back as he tells Dad about growing up in Colombia. I do take it in, but the shivers running up and down my back are a little distracting.

By the time we go in for supper, I'm as relaxed as I ever get around my parents.

Until it's time for us to go to bed.

Of course, they don't put him on the sofa, now that they know he's their future son-in-law. That's why we're facing each other in my childhood bedroom.

I have to say, they have made the shift from Matt to Rafael rather easily. Maybe they really did dislike him as much as I suspected. 'Sorry, this is awkward,' I tell Rafael. Because we might be about to walk down the aisle together, but we're virtually strangers.

'Don't worry, I'll sleep on the floor if there is an extra pillow and blanket. I don't mind at all.'

He really doesn't seem to. Problem solved. We're getting good at this.

'Hold on. Before we mess anything up.' I take out my phone. 'Our first night together in my parents' house.' It'll make a nice pic in front of my bed. #toocuteforwords.

But Rafael is too tall to fit comfortably in the frame with me and still get the bed in. I'm not about to take out my selfie stick in front of him again. 'Squat down a bit. A bit more. Lean back. No, back more . . . This isn't working.'

'How about this?' Before I know what's happening, Rafael has flung me onto the bed. He bounces down beside me. 'There,' he says, putting his head beside mine on the pillow. 'Lying down, we're an even match.'

They say the camera doesn't lie, but, laughing into the lens as I try not to drop it on our faces, we look as if we've been together for ages.

'One more. Wait.' I peel back the duvet and climb in.

'Come on.' His body is warm next to mine as we cuddle together. We pull the duvet up to our chins. 'Perfect,' I say, catching the moment. And I mean that. Rafael really is turning into the perfect fake fiancé.

Chapter 4

He will not stop waving that pale, flaccid abomination in my face. Talk about going against all that's civilised.

'What, never?' Rafael asks. 'Not even once, just to see if you like it? You might like it. How old are you, twenty-seven? And never tried it even once?'

'Get that thing away from me! No, never. I thought you were a nice bloke, but you're just like the rest.' I can't even look at it.

He laughs as he slurps down the oyster.

'That's still alive, you know.'

'Mmm, fresh. You're sure?' He holds out another one.

'Disgusting.'

'But how can you be from here and not enjoy what the sea offers, when it's caught *right there*?' He points at the glistening water beyond the restaurant's terrace. 'You won't even eat cooked shellfish like mussels? Clams? Prawns?'

'You can keep listing them off all you want. I'm telling you I haven't eaten any of them.' It's like I'm the only person in the world who's never been interested in shellfish. 'I won't like them.'

'How will you know unless you try? You could be depriving yourself of some of your favourite foods. What if it's as delicious as . . .' His lips twist as he thinks.

'Mini rice cakes with peanut butter,' I fill in for him. Then I nod at his expression. 'Yes, really. I even eat them for dinner. They're delicious, and don't knock them if you haven't tried them. Isn't that what you've just said?'

He laughs. 'When can I come over for dinner? I can't wait to try your rice cakes and peanut butter. That should pair perfectly with the bucket of water I'd need to unstick my tongue from the roof of my mouth.'

'What's your easy meal, then? And not takeaway, that's cheating.'

He doesn't hesitate. 'Pasta. I've always got some kind of bacon or salami or something in the freezer. A little olive oil, whatever veg is handy to roast, frozen peas in a pinch, and a bit of grated cheese.'

'Actually, that sounds good.'

'We can have your rice cakes and peanut butter as a starter. Maybe we'll invite your parents . . . Do they eat seafood?'

'They can't get enough of it.'

'Well, there you go.'

'There I go, what?'

'It proves that seafood is delicious.'

'No, it proves that some people like eating it. The same way I like my peanut-butter rice-cakes.'

He pops in another oyster.

'They look like the kind of thing I've seen runners cough up in the park, and I don't need to try that, either, to know I won't like it.'

He shrugs. 'I'm just saying that you're from Cornwall, and it is famous for seafood.'

I glance again at the fluffy clouds skittering above the terrace. The wind has whipped up the waves on the beach below us.

It's too hot to be out here, really. I've already gone to the loo twice to blot toilet roll under my arms. But we had to get out of the house this morning before Mum got the photo albums out. The less exposure to my parents that Rafael has, the better.

They are the UV rays of my life.

'You're from Bogotá but you don't deal drugs,' I point out, rather callously, 'so not everyone has to do what a place is known for.'

'Actually, there's something I should tell you . . .' he says. 'Kidding.'

He throws his hand in front of my phone as I aim it at his plate. Just because I'd never eat those things doesn't mean I can't Instagram them in all their slimy glory. #notinamillionyears.

'What are you doing?' I delete the blurry photo of his palm.

'What are *you* doing?' He watches me snap a few selfies with the restaurant behind me and then backdropped against the sea beyond the terrace railings.

'Taking pictures for my social-media accounts. Remember? Part of the plan?'

'Fine, take your photos, but you're only going to take the piss out of those poor oysters, no?'

'And you,' I tell him. 'What better way to introduce my readers to our story? A romantic lunch with my new fiancé. Get your hand out of the way. That's better. Don't worry, you're not in it. Well, you are, but you're blurry. See? I'll start with the photos this weekend and ease into some outtakes from the magazine story starting next week. You are okay with this, right? Because it's really important.'

'It's fine, Nelly, don't worry, take as many as you want. Sorry I got protective over the oysters. I didn't want their feelings to be hurt if you took their bad angle.'

'How caring you are,' I say.

He makes a heart out of his fingers. That man is an Instagram natural. I can't wait till I can post pics.

Matt never let me post about him. I couldn't even use his name. He's known only as BF (boyfriend) on my blog. At first I wondered if maybe I could just swap Matt for Rafael, like the substitutes that Tesco does in my online shop. Sorry, we're out of stock of your usual boyfriend, so we've sent this Colombian Supremo instead. But that won't work because Martha is going to start with how we fell in love despite me already being engaged.

It's all got to come out. Carefully managed, of course,

but out nevertheless. I've already written the blog post. It goes up first thing in the morning.

I doubt I'll sleep much tonight.

This isn't a big birthday for Dad, but my parents do love an excuse for a party. All their neighbours are here, but luckily Gran isn't coming and my brother is still working in Abu Dhabi, so Rowan is back in London with the children. Not that I've got anything to worry about with Rowan. She understands this family. I know she'll back up my story. We've told the children that I was hibernating on their sofa because I'd dumped Matt, not the other way around.

Naturally, my parents' friends all want to meet Rafael. Even if he wasn't such a looker, some of them knew Matt, at least by reputation, and everyone is dying for gossip about Sheila and Bob's daughter. Not to blow my own trumpet, but I've been their main source of entertainment since I first failed all my A levels. I'm now a cautionary tale in this part of Cornwall. How Not to Live Your Life. Updated and reprinted annually, it seems.

Don't believe me? Let me give you the highlights so far, starting soon after I moved to London.

I got a call from Microsoft about someone trying to hack into my computer. Can you believe it?! Well, I did. The scammers got into my bank account online and cleaned it out. Dad had to loan me two thousand quid. I would have paid it off quicker if I hadn't got fired from my first job after accidentally 'replying all' to my work friend on a particularly colourful boss-bashing email. And that wouldn't have been so bad, except that it meant I was home during the day in my shared flat when the police raided it, looking for my housemate. That was my housemate, the drug dealer. I thought she just had a very active social life. It all got cleared up, for my part, but not until I'd spent time being questioned.

That all happened within my first year of moving to London. Let's just say I haven't slowed down since.

Well, for once I'm coming off as the winner.

Ha, I laugh in the face of your unconvincing concern and shrug off the little digs about how sad it is that things didn't work out with Matt. Oh no, don't pity *me*, for behold my even better fiancé!

But the men whisk him off while I'm stuck fielding questions from their wives. By the time I find him in the kitchen with Dad, it's too late. Dad's got the shot glasses out.

'What are you doing?' I hiss at Rafael. I should have warned him that alcohol can send Dad down some strange paths.

'Having a drink with your father. Here, have one.' He pours another shot.

'That's not a good idea.'

'It was his idea.'

I bet it was. 'Dad, go easy, will you?'

'Woah, Nelly, lighten up.' He goes into hysterics at that old chestnut.

It's worse than I thought. But when I go to find Mum, she's not interested in coming inside because she's too busy smoking in the garden with her friends.

What are my parents, fifteen years old?

By the time I get back into the house, Dad has Rafael in a headlock. 'Come on, try to break it, son. Really try. Aw, you're not trying. Don't go easy on me just because it's my birthday.'

I shake my head when I catch Rafael's eye. How was he to know that this is Dad's favourite party trick? It should have been in the family briefing under the headline: ways to be humiliated by my parents.

He ignores my warning and starts to struggle. That's what Dad's been waiting for. With the agility of a ballet dancer, Dad pulls Rafael's arm behind his back, flips him around and pins him to the ground.

Unfortunately, Rafael is a bigger bloke than Dad is used to wrestling. As his free hand flails to help right himself, it catches the edge of the worktop, then sweeps across it.

Dad's birthday cake, all three buttery layers of it, plops on the linoleum.

For just a second, there is stunned silence. Dad's friends are used to the show, but not quite such a big finale.

Dad lets go of Rafael, who immediately cradles his hand.

'Mum is going to murder you,' I tell Dad. 'She ordered that especially from Mary's. Are you okay?' I ask Rafael.

'Your dad's got a good grip,' he says. Then he gets to his

feet and, with his right hand clasped against his chest for safety, sticks his other one out to shake. 'Well done.'

Dad ignores the gesture, pulling Rafael in for a hug. 'Welcome to the family.'

'Thanks. Could I please have some ice?' he murmurs.

I have to step around the pile of smeared icing to get to the freezer.

This is going about as well as I'd hoped.

Chapter 5

Text from Rafael:

I had an amazing time with you. I feel like I am dreaming, I loved every single minute so much. But it's not a dream. I never thought I could be this happy and I cannot wait to see you again. xxxxx R

'You're blushing!' Mum cries. 'That's from Rafael, I assume?'

'Yeah.' But my red face isn't for the reason she thinks. I read the text again. Surely he'll realise he's sent it to the wrong person when whoever that was meant for doesn't reply. And then he'll be as mortified as I am. I stare again at his words. I have to answer, to let him know.

Really sorry, but you sent this to me by accident. Nelly

My mobile rings seconds later. ''scuse me a sec,' I tell Mum. The wedding-dress shop isn't huge, so I tuck myself behind a rail of frocks. 'Hi, Rafael.'

'It wasn't an accident,' he says. 'Those words are meant for you.'

In that case, it might be the nicest text I've ever had from a bloke. Wow. He did seem to enjoy himself, but I had no idea he loved the weekend *that* much.

I did too. Even knowing we had to fool my parents and all of their friends, I wasn't quite the bundle of nerves I usually am when Matt and I visit. When Matt and I used to visit. 'Well, thank you. I'm looking forward to seeing you again too.'

'Put it in a text,' he says. 'Back to me. And you should delete the one you just sent.'

Oh, God. Of course he didn't mean what he said! It's part of our agreement.

And I've just told him I want to see him again. For real. 'Good thinking, I'll text you now.'

'I figured we should have as much evidence as we can about the relationship, especially since we don't have any from before.'

'We've got a good reason for that,' I remind him.

'And now we have a good reason for loved-up texts. Sorry, I won't keep you any longer.'

'No, okay, bye. I will text you back, though only when I'm done here, okay? Bye.' I've got enough to worry about right now without inventing a loved-up message for my faux fiancé.

I can do this. I *can* do this. It's not necessarily a bad idea to meet Rafael's best friend and deal with my mother *and* shop for my wedding dress while nosy cameras document the whole thing. That's what this is all about anyway. Now that it's no longer about love or happiness, I mean.

A normal bride would have done this months ago, but Martha was very clear that they'd want to follow some of the planning. It's okay, though, because this shop can get a dress in about two weeks. I just have to pick one.

Today should be one of the happiest days of my twenty-seven years and yet all I want to do is go back to Rowan's slippery sofa for a good cry. Because I'm not happy, am I? I'm pretending bliss to everyone I know, and lots of people that, until this morning, I didn't know.

It's true what they say. Social media is a total con job. Instagram lives aren't real and nobody is truly that Facebook fabulous. Take my blog. The big reveal posts I did about Rafael (ta da!) have gone bonkers with gushy comments about how lucky I am. I've not only dodged a bullet (said some) but found actual true love.

And now I'm getting packages nearly every day from wedding companies. They do this. They send samples to bloggers and Instagrammers in the hopes that their product will be featured. This morning I got a box of chocolate bars with our names on the wrappers. I snapped a dozen photos before I sampled every single one. If Rafael is lucky, he might get a square or two. Maybe.

The thing is, I'm a fraud. The only thing stopping me from confessing that I didn't know Rafael existed until two weeks ago, or that I've been more intimate with my dentist (which is fine; that's not in the agreement), is the horrible thought that if I do, everyone will know that I've been romantically judged and found wanting. Plus, now Rafael's fate is tied up with mine. I wouldn't want to ruin his life just because I routinely ruin mine.

I'm just about to start on another glass of the shop's free bubbly – which isn't mixing very well with the chocolate – when the door opens.

'*That's* his best friend?' Mum murmurs from behind her champagne flute. 'Goodness.'

'I guess so.' When Rafael talked about his bestie, Mabs, I pictured a Babs. You know, the kind of woman you'd describe as a good laugh, the life of the party, but never Britain's Next Top Model.

Rafael didn't mention that he was friends with a Colombian Gisele.

I swear the next few moments happen in slow motion. Mabs strides through the door, pushing her sunglasses up into her long, perfectly smooth honey-blonde hair and dazzling everyone with a kilowatt smile that could power the National Grid. Her huge eyes glint in her sun-kissed face.

But that's not even the most stunning part of her, because she's also got legs all the way up to her cleavage.

'I'm sorry I'm late!' Her voice is rich and throaty as she embraces Mum, then me. I bet she'll have a sexy laugh. 'You are Nelly who has captured Rafael's heart.' She holds me at (tanned, fit) arm's length, making me wish I hadn't started sweating like a marathon runner. '*Chica bonita.*'

'Thank you,' I say, because that sounds like a compliment.

'And this is Martha, from the magazine. I think Rafael mentioned it?'

She takes Martha's hand first, then waves to the cameraman. He hasn't stopped filming since she walked through the door. I can't fault his artistic eye. Mabs definitely makes a better subject than me and Mum bickering over whether I should wear my hair up or down.

'Yes, the series,' says Mabs. 'How romantic and lucky that you're able to carry on with Rafael, no? For the story, I mean.'

I'm searching her words, her expression, for any sign that she's suspicious.

'It's super lucky,' Martha says. I'm glad to see that I'm not the only one feeling completely outshone by Mabs. Martha is straightening bits of her wavy dark hair. Then I see her rub her lips together before she continues. 'But most lucky for Nelly to have found Rafael in the first place! I'm over the moon for her.'

I believe she really is. When I rang to tell her about the change in groom I could barely get the news out, what with all the oohing and aahing that she did. This is the perfect assignment for a gushy romantic like Martha.

Mum scooches over so that Mabs can join us on the long sofa. If I'd worn a skirt that short, I'd be in constant fear of crotch creep, but Mabs is lounging like she's in jogging bottoms. That's a woman who's used to wearing hardly any clothes. I can't stop staring at her bare legs as she crosses them.

'Well, Mabs,' says Mum, 'it's lovely to meet you. We are so excited for Nelly and Rafael.'

Oh, I could kiss her for that. She does sometimes back my corner. She might feel perfectly free to rubbish me, but that's her fiercely guarded territory.

'Tell me,' she goes on, 'how did you and he get to be such great friends?'

When Mabs sips her champagne, not a smidge of lipstick smears the rim of her glass. They can't really be that berry colour. Can they? 'We met in London,' she says. She's acting like she doesn't even know the camera is there. Every time my eyes dart towards Martha, she has to remind me to act natural. I can hear the cameraman sigh each time. 'I don't remember exactly how,' Mabs adds. 'Through friends, I guess, at a party or a club. It seems he's always been in my life.' Her laugh rings with smutty fun, just as I suspected. 'We are soulmates.'

'How nice,' Mum says, giving me a knowing glance.

Caroline, the shop owner, stalls any more of Mum's interrogation when she wheels out a chrome rail hung with dresses. 'It's time!' she says.

'We do not get to choose them for her?' Mabs asks.

'Oh, I've already told Caroline which styles I think I might like,' I say, 'but I guess you could have a look too, if you want?' Caroline nods at my question. 'Meanwhile, I can start with these.'

Mabs bounces to her feet to peruse the other rails. Mum stays firmly on the sofa, with her eye on Mabs, while

Caroline comes with me behind the curtain to help me into the first dress. Most of these confections look like a two-woman job.

It's not a problem, per se, that Rafael's best friend is a woman, I think as Caroline starts on the first of a million buttons up the back of the dress. Why should it be?

I just wish I'd seen her before I promised to make her my bridesmaid, that's all.

Mabs calls to me through the curtain. 'Where are the others? Your friends? The other bridesmaids?'

'Oh. You're the only one.' I don't need to see her face to know she's definitely judging me as a Sally-no-mates now. 'It's only because, well, it's a long story.'

'Matt didn't want a big do,' Mum helpfully adds.

'Yes, thanks, Mum, though the less we talk about my ex while I'm trying on wedding dresses, the better, probably.'

Mum is right, though. It's a bit awkward, to be honest. Sort of a legacy issue. Matt started freaking out whenever I tried talking to him about our attendants, so eventually we settled on one each: my brother at his side and his sister at mine.

That probably should have been a clue. Most fiancés don't lose the plot when asked a simple question about who they'd like to stand up at their wedding. Even if the proposed best man *is* as elusive as a unicorn. Despite his constant work assignments abroad, Paul has promised he won't let me down on the day.

Agreeing to have only Matt's sister on my side has made

things tricky with my friends, though. I've been avoiding them because, even though they don't say it, it was kind of an insult not to be asked. It would be tasteless to do it now even though Rafael probably wouldn't mind a bigger wedding party. It's also best that we don't spend too much time together till after this is over. I'm afraid they'll wheedle the real story out of me if we do. Besides, despite the whole magazine thing, and my blog, we wanted a pretty low-key wedding.

We. I've got to stop saying that. There is no *we* anymore. It's just me and my pretend groom now.

I can feel my lip start to wobble. No. I will not cry while being buttoned into my wedding dress. That's too pathetic. Besides, now is not the time for that.

This is the time for me to get to grips with the fact that Mabs will be my bridesmaid. Ugh. The thought of having to follow her down the aisle, or worse, watch every eye swivel to watch her follow me, like I'm the warm-up act at my own wedding.

I suppose it's too much to hope that she'll get chickenpox on the day, or a thyroid condition that adds weight. I'm not asking for much. Only a few stone.

Mum is wearing her diplomatic face when I step from the fitting room. 'Hmm, that's nice,' she says.

'Right, I'll try the next one on.'

'Wait, let me get a good look at it,' Mum says.

'Why? You clearly hate it.' I'm not in love with it, either. There seem to be about eighteen layers of it around my middle.

'Let's see all the options,' she says. 'Those sleeves are nice.'

Cap sleeves or off the shoulder suit me. Maybe lacy sleeves. Not straps and definitely nothing strapless. I'd only spend the whole day worrying my boobs would fall out.

Mabs is appraising me from the dress rail. 'Rafael loves legs. Where are your legs?'

'Under the dress where they belong,' I say.

'Are you ashamed of them?' With that she strides to me, grabs a handful of the (admittedly voluminous) skirt, and lifts it to waist height.

'Hey, easy on the exposure!' When my glance darts to the cameraman, I catch Martha's head shake.

'You have decent legs,' Mabs says. 'You should show them.'

'For the wedding?'

'Yes, why not? Don't be so stuffy. Is that really your style?' She's pointing at the dress, but I get the feeling she's asking about my personality too.

'Well, maybe not this exact dress, no. That's why I'm trying all these on, to see what I like.'

Mabs turns to Caroline. 'Have you got any short ones?'

Caroline straightens the jacket on her tastefully tailored trouser suit. 'No, I'm afraid we don't.'

'That's a shame.' Then she does turn towards the camera. She gives it a Meaningful Look.

It's fair to say that I'm not a fan of Mabs.

We may have sunk the entire bottle of free champagne by the time we leave the dress shop (success!), but now I'm not sure what to wear to my wedding (major fail).

Everything I thought I wanted got tainted by Mabs's judgement. I've got nothing against my legs, for the record, even though I don't choose to show off every single inch of them like she does.

I've got a good mind to make her walk up the aisle in a kaftan. And not one of those trendy, flowy, hippie ones, either. The kind that seventies housewives wore to hide their wobbles. Let the guests wonder what's underneath all that gaudy fabric.

She pulls out her mobile just as we're leaving the dress shop and starts talking a mile a minute to whoever she's rung. I can't even eavesdrop properly because I don't know more than two words of Spanish. The only word I catch is *cariño*. Judging by the way she keeps throwing her head back and laughing, it must be a boyfriend. Or a wannabe boyfriend.

Then she notices that Mum and I are about to go in the opposite direction, towards the Tube. She puts her hand over her phone. 'Rafael's just finished football practice. He wants to know how it went. Good, yes?' She's smiling like we couldn't be better friends.

Now I'm really not a Mabs fan.

Chapter 6

Martha keeps staring at us like we're the last crème brûlée on the buffet. She's so greedy for our story that she's practically salivating. Though Rafael might have something to do with that, since he's looking particularly good. It's hotter than a pizza oven in my flat, yet he seems naturally air-conditioned. It must be his Colombian-ness, being raised where it's hot. I assume it is hot, though I should probably know that for sure, given that I'm about to marry the man.

His flowered shirt isn't even stuck to his back like the rest of ours are. He's actually got jeans on! The only concession he's making to the temperature is that he's got his sleeves rolled up. I've changed my tee shirt twice already. I can feel my knees sweating all over the hem of my skirt. *Yes, Mabs*, I think, *knees*. I do show them when it's appropriate.

No wonder Martha is so keen for this. I've managed to stall most of her questions up till now with the tantalising promise of hearing it from the (new) horse's mouth.

Yet I can't stop thinking about the old horse. I'd give

anything for it to be Matt sweating beside me right now. Instead, he's sweating in another time zone, maybe even with another woman.

Is that really why he backed out? That uncomfortable piece of grit has been rubbing away at me ever since his email. When he said he wasn't ready to get married, maybe he meant he wasn't ready to get married to me. His future wife might be a windsurfing, sangria-drinking beach babe.

Martha breaks into my thoughts before they get any darker. 'I don't want to focus too much on background,' she tells us both as we're perched on my sofa, 'since the piece needs to be a fly-on-the-wall account of the run-up to the wedding. But I'd love a kind of he said/she said account of how you met. Especially because it wasn't the original story.'

'But you're not going to talk about . . . the original story, right?' I say. Now my knees are really sweating. 'Because we agreed that Matt is outside the scope of the piece now.' I might not be able to get him out of my head, but I don't want him in this story. The last thing I need is for him to start telling everyone what really happened.

'Oh, no, absolutely not,' Martha assures me. 'We'll position it as a fabulously romantic whirlwind between you two.' Her look is expectant. 'So?'

'So, you want to know how we met,' Rafael says. 'Naturally.' He leans back on the sofa and stretches out his legs. 'It was simple, really. She walked into my office and in that first minute, she stepped straight into my heart.

Until that moment I didn't know there was room for so much love. No, more than love. Adoration, admiration, excitement. Peace.'

I grab his hand because, I mean, wow. That could earn first prize in the competition for the cheesiest lines ever uttered by a bloke (subcategory: who's not wearing socks), and yet . . . It's not just my make-up that's starting to melt.

Better yet, he's staring at me like I really have climbed into his heart. Martha is eating it up.

I know perfectly well that this is all for show, but it's uncanny how real it can feel, especially when we're close like this. #wow.

What's most confusing is that, real or not, I sort of like hearing Rafael saying these things. It can't be right to feel that little twitter of excitement, not after being so in love with Matt. Even if he deserves a bollocking much more than my love.

He would have hated being here today, and he wouldn't have bothered hiding it, either. I didn't love that about him. He could be a real pain in the arse when he didn't want to do something that I did. More often than not, I'd just go on my own rather than risk his grumpiness ruining my evening too.

'What did you think when you first saw Rafael?' Martha's question pulls me back to the sofa. No reason to be thinking about Matt now, not when her pen is poised to catch whatever joyous romantic tale I'm about to utter about Rafael.

'I thought he was . . .' I'm about to say cute. I can't say cute. I'm not twelve. Come on, Nelly, think.

But everything that pops into my head sounds too trite. I'm no good at this romantic stuff.

Then I get another idea. Rafael isn't the only one who can make an impression. Martha wants a story. She's going to get one. 'I thought he was full of himself,' I say, ignoring his surprised expression. 'I'd gone upstairs to sort out a problem. A problem caused by Rafael because he'd messed up an account.' I'm warming to my theme now. This is good, not to mention *on brand* when it comes to my blog which is, after all, why I'm going through all this.

'I did not mess up an account,' he says. He's actually looking affronted.

'You did. You just wouldn't admit it.' Turning to Martha, I say, 'See? He won't admit it. Anyway, I'd left messages but he never called me back.'

'That's because I didn't know how charming you were,' Rafael says. 'Otherwise I would have.'

'It's because you knew you were in trouble. I finally had to go upstairs to catch him in person.'

'She was extra beautiful when she was angry,' he says, laying it on thick now.

'He pretended to need the loo,' I add. 'To escape.'

'I had to get control of myself.' He is looking a little flushed now.

'Because you were afraid of me,' I quip back. I must stay in character even if his eyes *are* boring into mine. They're such a deep brown that they're nearly black. I'll tell you this: anyone who could temper chocolate to that kind of rich shine would be Star Baker on *The Great British Bake Off*. 'I camped out at his desk until he came back,' I say, instead of dwelling on Rafael's eyes. 'His phone was there, so I knew he had to come back eventually.'

'I didn't take long,' he says. 'And I fixed your problem easily.'

Damn. Just when I was having fun with that storyline. 'But then I looked into all of his accounts and realised he'd done them all wrong. He had a lot of fixing to do.'

'Which meant she had to keep talking to me.'

'On purely a professional level.'

'Speak for yourself,' he says. 'I was completely, hopelessly, madly in love with you already, *mi corazón*.'

'I— Erm, well, I was otherwise engaged, literally, as you know.'

'I knew. I waited.' His smile oozes adoration. 'I would have waited a lifetime, as long as I got to be near you.'

If I didn't know for absolute sure that he was doing this for his passport, *I'd* believe him.

Martha has her chin in her hands. 'You must have known too, Nelly. You've practically got sparks coming off you!'

Do I? 'I can honestly say that when we met, I had no idea whatsoever that we'd be here right now, but as soon as I realised, I couldn't imagine anything stopping us.' True, every word. Absolutely true.

'And now we are here, no?' Rafael finishes. When he puts

his arms around me, I nestle into him. He smells like pine trees. Not floor cleaner. Cedar. Nice. 'About to be married.'

'Wow, well, thank you,' Martha says. 'I think we'd better leave you two alone now! The readers are going to love this so much.'

As soon as I close the door on Martha, who goes off to start writing our love story, Rafael and I grin at each other. 'We did it!' I say. 'You're a good liar.'

'Thank you very much. So are you. Remind me to have you make my excuse the next time I want to avoid my mother.'

'You can count on me,' I say. 'I'm an expert at mother-avoidance.' Then something occurs to me. 'Have you told your parents? About us?'

His smile is lazy and quite wonderful, really. 'Us?'

'I–I mean the plan.'

'I have told them about us. I have told them that I've met the most amazing woman. That you are an inspiration to me, a multi-talented, caring individual who is so full of heart that I can't imagine how I lived before we met. I have told them that I love you now and always will, and that I can't wait to spend the rest of my life being happy together.'

'Erm, thank you. That was very nice of you to say.'

He's still got his eyes locked on to mine. 'You're welcome.'

Get over yourself, Nelly. This isn't real. 'Right, because I guess everyone has to hear the same story or this won't work. Sorry I painted you as the bad guy before, with Martha. Only a bit, though. I think she likes the differences.

Maybe we should play that up. It's Martha's job to guide the series, but it wouldn't hurt to give her a few suggestions. It's my publicity, at the end of the day.'

When Rafael glances at his phone, it feels like a light going off. 'Whatever you like,' he says. 'This is your show.'

Back to business it is, then. 'Let's definitely play up the differences. It makes things more interesting.'

'I think it's pretty interesting now,' he says, tucking away his mobile. 'Don't you?'

I laugh. 'Well, I didn't expect to be marrying a stranger, that's for sure, so I guess so. It's weird, isn't it? To be pretending such an intimate thing when we don't even know each other.'

'We can change that,' he says. 'We'll do a crash course in each other. Nelly 101.' He pretends to take a pencil from behind his ear and poises it above his imaginary notepad. 'Nelly, what's your middle name?'

'Elizabeth.'

'Nelly Elizabeth Fraser—'

'Helen, actually.'

He looks confused. 'Is it Elizabeth or Helen?'

'It's Helen Elizabeth. Nelly for short.'

'We're lucky Martha didn't ask me that trick question.'

'Or anything trickier, like my favourite breakfast or my bra size!' *Bra size?! What the hell are you talking about?*

He politely ignores my foot in my mouth, though I catch his smirk. 'Helen Elizabeth Nelly-for-short Fraser, how do you spend your free time?'

'Free time? What's that?' I say. 'I'm working all the time. Even during work-work, I'm checking my accounts and answering messages.'

'I won't tell your boss.'

'I don't think spouses are allowed to testify against each other.'

'I don't think that rule applies to grassing on colleagues who are supposed to be processing my clients' claims.'

Oh, right. Possibly not the best confession to make to the person that I'm, indirectly at least, working for. 'I mostly do it at lunchtime.'

'Sure you do,' he says. 'Is that why Jenny had to tell me there was a delay on my latest claims?'

'Erm, no.' It totally was. 'Anyway, what do you do in your free time? Let's have a little Rafael 101.' And hopefully get off the subject of what I do during working hours.

'I read, go to the gym, salsa on Tuesdays—'

'The dance or the dip?'

He laughs. 'The dip is for every night, and it's more of a condiment, actually.'

'Condiment. Big word, I'm impressed with your English. Though of course it's miles better than my Spanish. Which is nil. What's condiment in Spanish?'

'*Condimento*.'

'You're joking. Is that all Spanish is? Adding an "O" to the end of words?'

'You've cracked it.'

'That's easy-o, then. Anything else that you do?'

'There's also Fantasy Football, real football. Oh, and coaching my kids. Does that count as a free-time activity?'

'Do you get paid?'

'No,' he says.

'Then it counts. You're making me look very lazy. I sometimes watch box sets after work. Do you watch any?'

'No, but I would if you wanted.'

An image of Rafael and me cuddled together under a blanket on my sofa pops into my head. Clearly *that's* not going to happen. 'Coffee or tea drinker?'

'Please, Nelly, I am Colombian.'

'Fine. How do you like your coffee?' I ask.

'Espresso with two spoons of sugar. Are you offering me coffee?'

'I only have instant. I'm a tea drinker.'

'How did we ever fall in love with each other?'

After a split second, I laugh with him.

'Okay, do you need me for anything else?' he asks.

'Erm, no. Unless you're hungry? I was just going to get some Thai from around the corner. Their duck curry is delicious.'

'No, thanks. I've got plans later for dinner.' He must notice my face because he says, 'That's not against the rules, is it?'

'I don't care what you do with your personal life, technically. I was just thinking – if it's a date – what would happen if Martha saw you.'

He laughs. 'What are the chances of that?'

'Where's your date?'

'In Dalston. That's where I live, remember?'

'I remember. Where does Martha live?' He shrugs. 'Then how do you know she won't see you?'

'Because she won't be in my flat.'

'Ohhh. Oh, I see. *That* kind of date.'

'I can cancel if you want. It's nothing serious.'

I think about the poor woman who's probably waxing as we speak. 'No, don't do that. Have fun. Just be discreet, okay?'

'What happens in *mi casa* stays in *mi casa*.' He laughs at his joke and kisses my cheek.

'See you at the wedding food thingy?'

'Are you speaking Spanish?' he asks. 'I think you'll find that it's thing-o.'

'You're kidding!'

'Yes, kidding. Thursday after work,' he confirms.

We both listen to my tummy grumble, a long digestive, *juicy* sound. 'Sorry, hungry.'

'This early?'

'I suppose you eat at midnight.' Another difference between us. 'That's bad for you, you know. Earlier is better.'

He smiles. 'I don't always do what's good for me.' With that, he lets himself out.

I grab the Thai Palace takeaway menu, even though it's always the same order. But just as I'm about to make the order, I realise that red duck curry, chicken pad thai and green papaya salad is way too much food for one person.

Matt and I always shared it. Now I'll only have sad little leftovers from my meal for two.

'Twenty minutes,' the owner says.

'Thank you,' I choke out between tears.

Chapter 7

'What are you doing here?' I hiss at Rafael. I mean, I know he works here too, so it's obvious why he's in the building. It's just not obvious why he's standing beside my desk when Jenny will be back from the café any minute. It is *not* in the plan to tell her about us yet. 'We're not meeting till after work. *At* the food thingy.'

'Nice to see you too.' He's dressed the same as he was the night we met: white dress shirt, tie, suit. I pull at the lapel of my suit jacket. It's not one of my most flattering.

'Yes, hello. It's not that,' I tell him, hoping nobody has clocked him.

As if they wouldn't. The highlight of our day in this office is usually when someone opens a new packet of biscuits in the kitchen. You should see the excitement then. 'It's just that we're not public yet.'

'So? Let's be public.' Now it's his turn to whisper. 'We need a history together, remember?'

'Yes, I know. We did that at my flat already with Martha. Remember? I walked into your heart?'

'That's for you,' he says. 'This is for me.' Then he beams towards the office door where Jenny is coming in with our hot drinks.

'Well, this is a surprise. Hi!' she says, kissing his cheek while she stares at me. 'What brings you down to the little people's floor?'

He makes a ta da gesture at me. 'This little person, actually,' he says. 'We've got something to tell you.'

Jenny is rightly looking suspicious. She'll never buy whatever it is he's about to spring on her. 'Maybe this is better left till later?' I murmur to him.

'I can't wait any more,' he says. And then he pulls me into an embrace, right there in front of my entire office. Several people are watching us, as if Mr Kipling himself was handing out his tastiest cakes. 'Jenny, we lied to you the other night. When we met. When you thought you introduced us. We've known each other for quite a while. *Quite* a while.' As if Jenny could mistake what he meant by that.

She hands me my mint tea. 'You and Rafael? Really? But then that means . . .'

This is exactly why I don't want to have this conversation in front of our entire office. Everyone knows I was engaged to Matt. Now they all know (or think they know) that I was playing away. This won't do my reputation any favours. 'We fell in love, yes,' I tell her. Hopefully that will knock things on the head. I'd like to knock Rafael on the head right now.

'We've told our parents,' Rafael says, 'so now we can tell our friends. Obviously we have to, or you might not be free for the wedding.'

'YOU'RE GETTING MARRIED?!'

What? Since when are my colleagues invited to the wedding?

Everyone is now standing up for a better look. I could die. Or at least pull the fire alarm to clear the floor while I figure out how to spin this.

But I haven't got time, because Jenny is staring at me with her mouth open. I've got to say something. 'I know it seems like it's all happening quickly, but we've been . . . we've known each other for months. And since the deposits are already paid for the venue and such, we thought, why not? Crazy, I know!'

'Crazy wonderful!' she says, scooping us both up into her arms. 'I'm happy for you,' she murmurs into my ear. 'Now I understand why you had to end things with Matt. It makes perfect sense. And you! You know I love you,' she says to Rafael. 'Wait a sec. *This* was why you haven't brought anyone out with us in months! Because you've been holed up with Nelly all that time. And your mysterious weekend away . . . now I get it!'

And now I get it. Panic over. Rafael isn't inviting my whole office. He's only friends with Jenny and her boyfriend.

Rafael holds up his hands. 'You got me. I couldn't tell anyone about this incredible woman until she was ready. Now I want to shout it from every rooftop.' His deep brown eyes gaze into mine. But as I smile back, I'm wondering who he went away with. Not that it's any of my business.

I suppose I do need to know where he went, though, since I'm supposed to have been there too.

By the time I get to the food expo to meet Rafael, I'm exhausted from pasting the smile on my face in the office all afternoon. He got the luxury of rushing off to a client meeting after detonating his news bomb. I'm the one who had to grin through all the fallout.

He's supposed to be here somewhere.

It's an echoey cavern of a place, with identical white food tents set up in rows, like that big arms-dealing expo at the ExCeL Centre that everyone protests, except we're here for canapés instead of cruise missiles.

I'm packed in amidst wall-to-wall couples. Not like the bridal show Mum and I went to a few months back. There was barely a testicle in that room, just buckets of champagne, miles of silk, tulle and lace, and enough mother-daughter bickering to keep the whole country's psychologists in business. Speaking for myself anyway.

Reception food must be one of those things that couples are supposed to do together, like picking the venue and the band.

The venue. That was one of the first big decisions Matt and I made together. After deciding to get married, that is. Just remembering my excitement as we walked into the old 1930s filter house next to the reservoir . . . I knew that was where I wanted to promise to spend the rest of my life with him.

But that's all gone now, and I can't give in to those feelings now. Boo hooing won't bring him back. Must look forward.

I have got things to look forward to. Not anything to do with my love life, mind you, but still. Just this morning I got an email from another brand who wants to work with me. I'm not sure how much use I'd really get out of an exercise bike when my actual bike has been sitting in my hallway gathering dust for at least a year, but the point is that all this extra exposure is doing its job. I'll probably politely decline the bike. I'd only have to ride the thing if I accepted it. Worse, I'd have to photograph myself doing it.

It's not only the companies who are getting in touch. Smiling, I scroll again through my emails.

Dear Nelly,

You probably get a million emails like this, and I don't expect an answer back, but I just wanted to tell you what your blog means to me. I'm in the middle of chemo treatment for breast cancer. It's a nightmare – needles and cold caps and so much waiting and boredom! I don't know why it surprises me, since I've already been through it with my mum and my older sister. Anyway, I was pretty fed up with the whole thing. I mean, what's the point, really. Like I said, fed up.

But something about your story changed my mind. Not that you're fighting cancer, but I think that negative stuff happening to us is like a cancer. It can eat away at you if you don't fight it. Hearing everything that's gone wrong in your life made me realise that, other than this cancer, I've been pretty lucky. And now you've found the love of your life, so things will only get better for you. For me too, I hope.

So I just wanted to say thank you for being so honest and letting us follow your story. For the first time in a long time, I feel positive about the future.

Good luck with your wedding! I'll be reading all about it!

Kindest regards,

Amy Brody

I really hope Amy will be okay. I'll definitely email her back tonight, when I've got time to devote to it. It never seems like enough when I get messages like this. Not after the woman has taken time out from chemo to write.

My fingers itching, I open Instagram. This morning's post is doing okay. Quickly I scroll through the comments, liking most and quickly answering a few.

'Talking to your adoring public?' Rafael asks as he sneaks up beside me. Then he kisses my cheek, which seems ridiculously formal, surrounded by lovers as we are. Besides, we're supposed to *be* lovers. It's a good thing Martha's not here yet.

'Erm, we should probably kiss,' I tell him. 'When Martha is around, I mean.'

We haven't done the whole kissing thing yet. We'll have to at some point. It's not normal never to kiss in public (despite what Matt always preferred). People will get suspicious.

'For authenticity?' Rafael smiles. Then he moves until he's inches from my face. 'Like this?'

His lips slowly meet mine. They're soft and warm and they definitely feel authentic.

'That'll do,' I say primly. 'Yes.' #kneeslikejelly.

'Are you sure we shouldn't try again, just to make sure we've got it right?' He's got a way of smiling that looks like we're sharing an extra-special private joke. I find myself wanting to quip back, to keep this moment playing out. I want to be in on the jokes that are just for us.

'I don't remember practice runs being in our agreement,' I say. 'Did I get the whole contract?'

'Have your people talk to my people. I'm sure it was in my contract. I know a good clause when I see it,' he answers, keeping his eyes locked on mine.

I've got no witty reply. It's all I can do not to lunge at him again.

But I don't need to launch myself, because Rafael glances into the crowd just before he leans down, closes his beautiful eyes and kisses me again.

'Love birds!' cries Martha. 'Hold on. Do it again. Did you get that?' she asks the bloke pointing his lens at us.

'Authentic,' Rafael murmurs so that only I can hear. Then his lips meet mine again while the photographer snaps his picture. Hopefully he can edit out the extra pink in my cheeks. Or not. I am supposed to be the blushing bride after all.

He must have seen Martha. That's why he kissed me again. Maybe if I tell that to my heart enough times, it will stop thumping so wildly.

'Now, here's how it's going to work,' Martha says. She's all business now. She's tied her hair up in a messy bun to prove it, and she's peering at us from over the top of her wire-rimmed glasses. 'You do your thing as if I'm not here. I'll be following you around but not interfering. Oh, and Nelly? Try not to look at the camera. Matt wants candids for this story.'

Hearing the name gives me a jolt. Then she nods at the photographer. She doesn't mean my Matt. Even my Matt isn't my Matt any more.

I'd like to see you try to act natural when someone tells you to act natural. I'm aware of every awkward, stilted move I make. Each laugh sounds fake. And, of course, I can't stop looking at Photo Matt. Meanwhile, Rafael carries on as if he was born to have a camera following him around. He even grabs my hand before making a dash for the barbecue stall. His hand is warm and firm and doing nothing to calm the hammering in my chest.

What is wrong with me? You'd think a bloke has never held my hand before. Yet when Rafael does it, it feels as if all the air is being sucked from the room. It would explain why I'm feeling so giddy. This is *not normal*.

These must be rebound feelings. Of course. I've been on such an emotional roller-coaster these past weeks. Like an elastic band that's been stretched too far in one direction, now I'm hurtling too far the other way.

That's what this is.

'We get to eat as much as we want?' Rafael asks, collecting a little cardboard dish glistening with meat.

'That's what the ticket says. Though *that* wouldn't have been my first choice.'

'Mmm, *delicioso*.' He licks a blob of sauce from his lips. 'Try.' He holds an overloaded wooden fork out for me to taste.

'I'm supposed to put all that in my mouth?' Too late I realise how that sounds.

Rafael snorts. 'At least it's not an oyster. Or are you also against barbecue?'

I nibble a corner of the beef. 'It is good,' I admit. 'Though we can't serve barbecue.'

'Why not?'

'Because it's not wedding food. It's messy and ends up in your teeth.'

He takes another bite and closes his eyes with a sigh. Then he grins at me, saying, 'I don't know what you mean.'

He's managed to stick nearly the entire mouthful to his front teeth. 'Ugh, that's disgusting, and exactly my point. No barbecue.' He's still showing off his meaty smile. I will not encourage him. Even though I don't think I know of another person who would embarrass himself like that to make me laugh. 'I was thinking more like poached salmon with dill.' Now he's staring at me. 'What? Poached salmon is delicious. *Delicioso*, as you say.'

Rafael pretends to snore.

'It is not boring. It's very tasteful.' I don't tell him that it also goes nicely with the pastel theme I've been dreaming of. Think tumbling flowers and vintage teacups and oodles of romance. It's how I decorate my flat, and everyone knows how important it is to have a consistent theme, especially on Instagram.

Besides, we're having a wedding, not a rodeo.

He snores even louder. Then he says, 'Don't be so formal. Weddings are supposed to be fun, so we should have fun, no? We need fun food.'

I can't help but think of Martha lurking behind us. She's probably recording the whole thing.

What is fun food supposed to be, anyway? I can't think of any and, no, that doesn't make me unfun, for the record, which is where I can see this conversation heading. 'What's fun food?' I ask.

He counts off on his fingers. 'Tacos? Pizza? Nachos?'

'What is it with you and melted cheese? It's a wedding, Rafael, not a Friday night out with your mates. This is supposed to be a formal event.'

He clasps my hands in his. Looking deep into my eyes, he says, '*Mi corazón*, it's our wedding. This will be the moment when we tell everyone we know how much we love each other. That's a celebration, no? It can be anything we want. The only important thing is that we are there with each other. There are no other rules. There don't have to be. Come.'

With his warm hand enveloping mine again, he leads me down the first aisle. He marches straight past the delicate canapés, though. He turns his nose up at the mini eclairs and chocolate pots. What's he got against chocolate pots? 'Here,' he says, finally stopping in front of the end stand. 'Perfect.'

I roll my eyes at the donut display. 'Perfect for breakfast meetings, not so much for weddings.'

Just to spite me, I'm sure, he grabs a jelly-filled one and takes an enormous bite. 'Is that what Miss Manners says?' The filling oozes out, which he catches on his finger and perfectly proves my point.

I ignore the sticky bun he's waving in front of my lips. 'I suppose you think these are fine instead of a wedding cake.'

'I don't really like cake,' he says. 'Do you?'

'Of course I do, but that's not the point! Rafael, we've got to have a cake. What are we supposed to cut at the reception?'

He fishes a bamboo knife out of the little pot beside the donut display. 'Sweet, no?' When he saws through the jelly donut, a big splodge lands right beside his shoe. He deftly covers it with his sole and we move on.

'Now, *this* is more like it,' I tell him. Grabbing his hand,

I even manage not to look over at the camera.

I pull him over to the cake pop booth where hundreds of gorgeous pastel morsels are artfully displayed. Some are sprayed in silver or gold, others delicately drizzled with contrasting colours. They festoon the display tables, piled on to tiered dishes that give them a wedding cake look, or standing up in pretty flower pots, tucked amidst flowers in vases, or in champagne glasses (although that's a waste of a champagne glass, if you ask me). There are even ones decorated like tiny brides and grooms. 'Aren't they a feast for the eyes?'

Rafael accepts a pink-and-lilac-swirled pop from the woman at the booth. 'You're right. This would be much easier to cut than a donut.'

'At least it wouldn't dribble on the floor. We could have these as well as a little wedding cake.'

'If we can have a little wedding cake to cut,' he says, 'then we can also have the donut wall.' Then he sweeps me up into his arms. 'You are a problem-solver.' His lips are inches from mine. I'm not even blinking.

But instead of kissing me, he sets me down with a bump. 'If you let me have the donut wall,' he says, 'then we can get the cake pops too. It's all about compromise.'

'Where's the compromise in that when we both get what we want?'

'I know. I'm a great negotiator.'

With a devilish grin, he plants a kiss on the end of my nose before wandering further along the aisle. 'Mmm, smell that. Chilli! *Gracias*,' he murmurs, accepting from the attendant a small bowl piled with grated cheddar. 'Ah, this is really good. Here, try.' But when he holds the fork out to me, a drip of sauce flies off, landing on my boob.

'And that's why we're not having it at the wedding,' I say.

'Because your boob got in the way of my chilli?'

'Because your chilli will ruin my wedding dress. Besides, it's going to be a proper sit-down meal.'

'No, it's not, really?' He looks stricken at the very idea. 'Not sit-down. Those take so *long*. Plus you get stuck next to people you have nothing in common with, so nobody has as much fun.'

'Well, what do you propose? Hot dogs? Maybe a make-your-own pizza station? I know. We can order Dominoes and everyone can sit cross-legged on the floor wherever they like. My gran will need to double up on her arthritis pills, but it'll be worth it for that extra cheese and pepperoni.'

'I get the feeling you're teasing me.'

'No, Rafael, teasing is good-natured. I don't want people having to stand up to eat out of bowls. Besides, dogs eat out of bowls. I think we can do better for our guests than that. I'm not trying to be difficult. I just don't want to serve our guests anything they could get from a food truck outside their office at lunchtime. Could we maybe aim for a slightly higher bar?'

Martha is loving that we can't agree. 'Priceless!' she says again.

Rafael seems to notice her for the first time. He turns back to me and says, 'Of course we can, *mi corazón*. And I'm not trying to be *difícil*, either.'

'Not *difficulto*?'

'Not in this case, no, sorry.' He laughs. 'I love the way you always try to make our life so wonderful. Nelly, you are a treasure, and every day I wake, I appreciate my good fortune. That we found each other, that I found you. Thank you for being on this journey with me. I can't wait to eat donuts and cut wedding pops with you.'

As his lips find mine, Martha says, 'You two are a *dream* to work with!' Then I hear her murmur, 'You got that, right?' to Photo Matt, before raising her voice again. 'We're getting so much material, thank you. The only thing left is to get a few at-home shots, if that's okay. If you're free, we could do it quickly now. It would be nice for Matt to get a pic of you together on the sofa after your tasting, in total disagreement but still loving each other . . . You do still love each other?'

'More than ever,' Rafael says, pulling me to him. 'The joy this woman brings me every day, when I hear her voice, when I hold her hand, even when we disagree. It's immeasurable . . . Every moment is special when it is spent with you,' he says to me. 'We are a team after all, you and I. Right?'

'Right,' I say, puckering for another kiss as Photo Matt snaps his camera. 'Come back to the flat now. We haven't got any plans, have we?'

'Only to be together,' says Rafael.

Something flips again in my tummy. I'll take a couple of antacids when I get home.

Chapter 8

I haven't even kicked off my shoes when my doorbell buzzes. 'I'll just be a sec,' I tell Martha. 'Rafael, do you want to put the kettle on for everyone?' It's probably my downstairs neighbour. The delivery people always ring her bell if I'm not in. She doesn't mind taking in my packages, as long as I share some of the freebies I get with her.

'Hello?'

'It's me.'

What the actual fuck?!

'Matt!'

The photographer looks over, though I don't mean him. Martha glances at me too.

'Can I come up? I need to talk,' says Matt.

Why is there no volume control on this damn intercom? 'Erm, it's not really a good time,' I whisper. 'Can we talk later? Or tomorrow?'

What is happening? My entire plan is about to unravel spectacularly, that's what.

How dare he come here, now, after dumping me by

email! I've got to remember that. The man dumped me, his fiancée, by email. I've had more thoughtful kiss-offs from my internet provider.

He must have fried his brain in that Spanish sun if he thinks I want to talk to him.

'It's got to be now, Nelly. I'm coming up.'

Shite. Of course he can come up if he really wants to. He's got my key.

Martha is pretending not to notice anything wrong, but she's standing stock still. That's a listening-not-listening pose if ever I saw one.

I've got about thirty seconds to decide what to do.

Here are the facts. One: Matt dumped me, not the other way around like I've claimed, and it's very unlikely that he's forgotten that detail in the month we've been apart. Two: Martha *doesn't* know that Matt dumped me and not the other way around. Two (cont'd, Part A): Martha thinks I broke up with Matt because of Rafael. Two (cont'd, Part B): she'll never believe that he forgot that fact, either. Three: Matt is going to be rightly surprised when he sees my new fiancé. And four: my thirty seconds are up, because there's a knock at the door.

Then I hear the key turn, just as Rafael comes out of the kitchen with our teas. His glance asks the question. I wish I had an answer for him.

And then, just like that, the thing I thought I wanted happens. Matt is standing right in front of me.

'Hi,' I manage. I'm not moving a muscle.

Neither is he. 'Hi.' His deep tan makes his hazel eyes look even lighter (and they're leonine as it is). His hair is longer than usual. It curls at the base of his neck. That kissable, now strictly off-limits neck. I don't recognise his shirt. That bothers me.

As my flat is tiny, he can't help but notice the extra people in it. 'This is Martha,' I say, 'and her photographer, Matt. Martha from the magazine. You remember. And this is Rafael. Rafael, Matt.'

The men nod at each other. Rafael still has our tea mugs in his hands.

Now Matt's face is asking questions too, like why would Martha from the magazine be here when there's no longer a wedding story to write about, and who the hell is the bloke making us tea?

'Welcome back,' I say, not making any effort to keep my voice neutral. Why should I? I wasn't the one who said *adiós* to our relationship.

'Can we please talk?' His glance bounces between Martha and Photo Matt and Rafael. He clearly doesn't want spectators any more than I do.

It's the perfect out! I'm giddy with relief that he hasn't said anything in front of Martha. 'Martha, do you mind?' I ask, though she's already nodding and gathering her things.

Rafael sets down our teas.

'Hang on,' I tell him. Because, if this was real, wouldn't I want my new fiancé here when my ex-fiancé turned up 'to talk'? 'Rafael needs to stay,' I add. 'Rafael, please stay. Thanks, Martha.'

Martha very much needs to go before she hears whatever Matt has to say.

'Not a problem,' she says. 'Then we'll see you Sunday at Chatsworth Market. We can meet you there. Is noon good?'

Rafael nods. 'Let's meet at the bottom end, by the Homerton Hospital. I'll need to shoot off for practice after.'

'Football practice,' I explain to Martha. 'Rafael coaches a boys' team. Two, actually.' I'm absurdly proud of this, as if he really is my boyfriend. I mean, fiancé.

Rafael grins at me. 'You're going to love the food at the market,' he says. 'You'll forget all about salmon.'

Now isn't the moment to point out my rule against food-truck meals.

'Excuse me, but what's going on here?' Matt asks.

Uh-oh. It's not the time for Martha to hang around either. 'I'll just walk them out quickly.' While I try to compose myself for the whopper of a tale I'm about to tell.

When we reach the door, Martha mutters, 'Awkward! Did you ever think he'd turn up like this? I hope it won't be too unpleasant for you. I suppose it's natural, even if you did make a clean break.' Her eyes search mine. 'Did you?'

'It couldn't have been cleaner,' I tell her honestly, smarting all over again from Matt's email. I must remember that now. He's brought all this on himself. 'He probably just wants to tie up some loose ends, you know, like getting some of his stuff back.'

Her look is knowing. 'As long as it's only his stuff that he wants back,' she says as I close the door.

Both blokes watch me come back into my flat. 'Well, this is a surprise,' I say. Every true sentence I can utter has got to be good for me. Not that I believe much in karma, but if it does exist, then I must be earning *some* credit.

'Same here,' Matt says, staring pointedly at Rafael. 'I expected you to be alone.'

He would, wouldn't he, when he dumped me. 'Sorry to disappoint you.' So much for my karmic credits for being nice. Actually, I'm not sorry at all. 'I guess I should tell you a few things.'

He crosses his arms. Something in that simple gesture, which is one of Matt's favourites, by the way, raises my blood pressure and makes me see red.

On the plus side, all the upset of the past months drains away from me until there's nothing left but the bare bones of my anger. *He's* put out?

'Nelly? Do you want to tell me who this is?'

He knows me well enough to know my furious smile when he sees it. 'Of course, Matt. This is Rafael, my fiancé. Martha was here to cover our wedding.'

'Your wedding!'

'Mmm hmm,' I say sweetly.

'You are joking.'

'Am I? Hmm, let me see. No, actually, I'm not. Rafael

and I are getting married. I'm sorry you had to hear it this way. It's probably a shock. Maybe even as big of a shock as I got when you dumped me by email.'

His expression is one of utter disbelief. 'I did not dump you! Nelly, all I said was that I couldn't go through with the wedding. That's all.'

'Would you ever want to go through with marrying me, Matt? Honestly?'

'Why can't we just be happy the way we are? You were happy, weren't you?'

'Yes,' I admit. 'But partly because I thought this was going somewhere. I thought you were committed.'

'I am committed! Look, I even had the chance to sleep with other people in Spain, and I didn't.'

He says this like I should give him a medal for not having sex straight after dumping his fiancée. 'Good for you.' Then I get an awful thought. 'What about other things?'

His look is suspicious. 'What do you mean?'

'You know, other things. Dates, late-night snogs. Early-night snogs?'

'That doesn't matter,' he mumbles. 'We were broken up. I—' He glares at Rafael, who's still standing beside me. 'Do you mind giving us some bloody privacy?'

Calm-as-you-like, Rafael says, 'I'm sorry, mate. That completely depends on what Nelly wants.' He does look genuinely sorry too.

'There's nothing you can't say in front of Rafael,' I tell Matt. 'He knows everything.' When I grasp Rafael's hand for effect, Matt flinches. My heart squeezes a bit, to be honest. 'I'm sorry, but . . .' I take a deep breath, because I have to do this. Even if Matt doesn't definitely want me out of his life, he did hurt me. No, worse, he ripped apart the trust I had in him *not* to hurt me. I know now that I could never be sure he wouldn't do it again. Even putting aside my feelings, Matt cannot know that Rafael and I aren't real. If he did, what's to stop him from telling Martha (and everyone we know) and then all this will really have been for nothing. I have to do this.

'You may as well know that I've known Rafael for months. We work together. Nothing . . . official happened until you broke up with me, but I love him.'

I know the tears that begin to swim in Matt's eyes aren't just for effect, but I have to think about myself now. He doesn't want to marry me, remember? Ouch.

'You love me,' he whispers. 'I know you do, Nelly. And I love you. Why are you doing this to me?'

'Doing this to you! You're the one who backed out of our wedding, Matt, not me.'

'You've just told me that you've been with him for months.'

That's right, I did. Hmm. In my revised version of events, Matt isn't actually the biggest arse here. This could be a problem. 'Well, yes, we knew each other, but it was platonic, as I said, until you dumped me. And, may I remind you, you didn't know about Rafael when you did that. So don't go pretending you were right to do it.'

'I didn't say I was right. I said I love you.' Ouch again. 'I don't know what this is,' he says, pointing at Rafael, 'but it's not love, not like we have.'

'It is.'

'It's not.'

'It is.' This is getting ridiculous.

Matt shakes his head. 'You don't have to take my word for it. I can prove it to you.'

'What do you mean? How do you plan to do that?'

'You'll see.' With that ominous threat, he chucks his spare keys on the sofa and lets himself out of my flat.

'Are you okay?' Rafael asks as soon as the front door closes. 'Do you want me to go?'

'I'm okay.' I take a shaky breath. 'I didn't like lying to him . . . hurting his feelings. Even though I shouldn't care after the way he treated me.'

'But of course you care, because that's the kind of person you are. It is completely his loss that he couldn't see what he had when he had you.'

I watch Rafael's expression. 'Are you just saying that? Is this real?'

'Why would you think I'm making it up? It's only us here, so yeah, of course it's real. I happen to think you're pretty great.'

'Sorry, I'm just not used to hearing it.'

'That's a shame, Nelly. You should be told it more often by the people who love you.'

His words hang in the air between us. Finally, he says,

'I'll leave you alone now, but ring me later if you want, okay?'

I am tempted later to ring, but what would I say? That I want him to tell me again how great he thinks I am?

My phone buzzes with Rafael's text while I'm brushing my teeth before bed.

Words can't convey what a wonderful woman you are, Nelly. I could try, but in this case even the dictionary is insufficient. You bring joy to me in every move you make and every word you speak. I'm going to do my best to make sure you know that every single day.

Taking a deep breath, I answer.

I never imagined I'd find someone who gives me such strength. Thank you for today. You've always got my back, and I'll always have yours. We make a great ~~team~~ ~~pair~~ ~~couple~~ *team.*

I know it's only more 'evidence' in case we need it later. I'm smiling anyway as I tuck myself under my cosy duvet.

Chapter 9

Martha has come over all Jeremy Kyle about this unwelcome turn of events.

'It's perfect!' she cried when I rang to apologise for Matt's interruption. 'Don't you see? Now we've got a real story!' I could practically hear her crackling with drama.

The trouble is, I don't want to star in my own soap opera. I simply want to fulfil the contract I've signed with the magazine, and the one that's implied with Rafael, so that I can get on with my life.

I haven't dared to breathe a word about Matt's reappearance on social media. What could I say that doesn't make me sound like a heartless rat? It was hard enough crafting the message in the first place. Believe me, it's a tightrope-fine line to walk between giving into the power of true love and plain old cheating. Of course Matt will win people's sympathy if they think he (the wronged party) has returned from licking his wounds in Spain (ha! He was licking something, I'll bet) to win me back.

Do you know what? I'm fuming. At the moment, that's

trouncing the hurt, which is probably a good thing because otherwise I'd probably do nothing but think about Matt and his Spanish snogging adventures. No matter what he claims, committed people don't break up with their fiancée and then run away to get off with random women.

I've done such a good job of constructing this story about me and Rafael that I almost have to remind myself that I haven't actually cheated. That this is all made up. Matt was the one who gave me the heave-ho while I was buying bridal magazines and trying to placate his mother about the floral arrangements. I didn't even know Rafael existed, let alone lust after him. It's Matt's fault that I'm about to go through a pretend wedding with a near-stranger.

Speaking of pretending, it's all I can do to keep the smile on my face when I see Mabs at Chatsworth Market on Sunday. She arrives with her arm linked through Rafael's. Even behind the sunglasses (large, glamorous) I can see that she has clocked me. She whispers something in Rafael's ear that makes him laugh. It takes all my self-assurance not to think it's about me. Of course I still think it's about me.

The market is heaving even though it's not sunny and, actually, the road is still wet from when it rained earlier. Take note, Mabs! You don't need those sunglasses.

It is so humid, though, that my hair, which normally stays where I've put it, is frizzing. Perfect for the camera, in other words.

'I missed you!' I tell Rafael, just before I land him with the sexiest kiss I know how to do. Go on, Mabs, I dare you to laugh at that.

When he sweeps me up in his arms for a hug, I can feel the muscles in his biceps bulging. I wish Photo Matt was here to capture it. Maybe we can re-enact it later.

But we won't need to. 'That's perfect!' Martha calls out as she emerges from behind a bratwurst stand. Photo Matt lowers his lens long enough to give us the thumbs up. 'Exactly what we're looking for,' she says. 'And we got lovely shots of you and Rafael coming up the road together,' she tells Mabs. Then she turns back to me. 'We'll do the same thing we did at the food fair and just stay in the background while you do your thing. Remember, try not to look at the camera.'

Mabs begins chattering a mile a minute to Rafael. 'Erm, sorry, Mabs,' Martha interrupts, 'but can you speak in English, please, while you're all together? Only because I don't speak much Spanish and I'll be eavesdropping!'

'Of course,' Mabs says. 'I was only saying how this used to be our favourite thing to do on Sunday mornings when we lived together. We've been coming here since it started, haven't we, *mi cariño*?'

I'm careful to keep my expression perfectly pleasant. Mabs and her *careenyo* lived together? As in *lived* lived together? Or just lived together? Either way, that definitely would have been useful to know before Photo Matt caught it all on camera.

'And now Rafael is sharing it with his fiancée, how romantic!' Martha says. I sneak a glance at her to see if she's purposely winding Mabs up, but I can't tell. 'Go on, wander around. Don't mind us.'

Rafael slips his arm over my shoulder, which means it's a squeeze for us to walk side-by-side amidst the crowd. Good, because that leaves Mabs to walk behind us.

When he leans down to plant a kiss on the side of my head, I have to twist around to glance up at him.

For just a second, while we stare at each other, everything around us falls away. It feels like seeing a beloved old friend after an absence, that moment when you plug back into each other and the current or connection or whatever it is runs between you again.

He curls me towards him so that he can tuck a lock of hair behind my ear. 'Now you'll get to taste some real food.'

Food, what food? I try to compose myself. 'What was that we ate at the food thingy, my imagination?' My heart is still set on the salmon, though I'd agree to the stuffed chicken if Rafael really hates the fish idea. It's stuffed with cheese. That ought to make him happy.

'Most of that was fiddly food to make an impression,' he tells me. 'This is food to fall in love with.'

Then the moment recedes as he leads us to a table piled with chocolate truffles in giant wooden bowls. It's like the stall was set up especially so people would take Instagram pics. It is so beautiful! #gainingweightjustlookingatthem.

'Mmm, three of these, please,' Rafael says. The woman

starts to put the cocoa-dusted treats into a bag. 'Please,' Rafael says, 'we'll have them now.'

She plonks one into my hand, then gives the others to Mabs and Rafael. When I bite into the crisp shell, a deep salty chocolaty goodness oozes onto my tongue.

'God, that's delicious.'

Rafael's cocoa-dusted lips meet mine for a truffley kiss. 'Told you.'

He's becoming awfully free with this kissing thing. Not that I'm about to complain. We've not discussed it, but it does lend authenticity to our story. People in love and about to get married do kiss a lot.

Then he turns to Mabs. 'Good, yes?'

'You know how I love these, *mi cariño*,' she says. 'Remember my birthday?'

They both laugh at some private recollection, which brings my mood down a bit. Why does she even have to be here? I'd be having a perfectly nice time with Rafael if it weren't for his best friend trying to steer him down her cosy memory lane every chance she gets.

'Nelly?' Rafael juts his chin towards the record stand.

I follow his gaze to find Matt standing beside the vintage Bee Gees vinyl. It takes me five furious seconds to reach him.

'What the hell are you doing here?'

'Waiting for you,' he says, like that's a perfectly reasonable answer.

'You shouldn't be here,' I say.

'Why not? This is open to the public, isn't it?'

'You know that's not what I mean.' I wish Mabs wasn't watching us. And Martha! Frantically, I look around. Yes, she's got her eyes trained on us too. 'There's no reason for you to do this.'

'That's where you're wrong,' he says. 'There's every reason to be here, because I love you.' Then he turns to Mabs. 'Hi, I'm Matt. Nelly's fiancé until a month ago.'

It's clear that Mabs couldn't be happier to hear this. She kisses both his cheeks with such enthusiasm that you'd think they were long-lost siblings. 'So very nice to meet you, Matt. I am Rafael's best friend. I had no idea about you.'

Martha has given up lurking behind the lunch options. She and Photo Matt join us.

'Really?' Matt answers Mabs as he turns to smile a *hello* at Martha. 'I'm surprised, since Nelly and I were planning our wedding until so recently.'

'And you're here, why?' Martha asks.

He doesn't take his eyes from my mortified face. 'Because Nelly is making a huge mistake and I love her too much to let that happen. Darling, you don't love this bloke. You can't, because you love me.'

'I think you should leave,' Rafael says, stepping in front of me. 'She doesn't want you here.'

Matt squares up to Rafael. 'That's up to Nelly to decide, not you, mate.' Then he says to me, 'Darling—'

'Don't call me that.'

'I'm sorry,' he says. 'We have a history together. Please give me a chance to make things right, because I made the biggest mistake of my life when I went to Spain. I should have stayed and talked things through with you. Maybe if I had, then this wouldn't be happening. Please, Nelly. Don't shut me out completely.'

'Even you must understand this,' he says to Rafael. Then he smiles at Mabs. 'You two were a thing once, right? Now she's your friend? Why can't I stay in Nelly's life too?'

When Mabs nods, I search Rafael's face. 'That was a long time ago,' he tells me.

So he and Mabs *were* a thing.

'Nelly?' Matt goes to reach for my arm but seemingly thinks better of it. 'Is it really so horrible to be on the same road as me?'

Everyone is watching me. 'Oh, I don't *care*. It's not going to change anything, Matt. I'm marrying Rafael.' With that, I take Rafael's arm and lead him away.

'Try to ignore him if you can,' Rafael whispers to me as we walk ahead. 'He can't hurt you if you don't let him. *I* won't let him.' There's that skittering in my tummy again.

His hand around mine is tighter than usual as we walk through the market. Or maybe that's my imagination. Either way, I'm grateful.

The tangy aroma of burning cheese (crepes) is making my mouth water. 'God, that smells good!'

Rafael sniffs the air. 'Which smell?'

'That cheese—' The word is out before I can stop myself. I clamp my lips shut.

Too late. He could not look happier to hear this. 'You mean the cheese from that food truck over there? Can it be possible that your heart is warming to my cheese theme?'

'It could be that I haven't had breakfast, and crepes are a perfectly normal thing to eat *in a market*.' There's no way I'm giving in that easily, even if my tummy is rumbling.

'You'll come around to the tacos,' he says. 'They have a freakish allure.'

'Never.'

'What if they did them with salmon?'

'No.'

'Your fancy chicken?'

'Nope.'

'What about caviar? Kobe beef? Fourteen karat gold shavings? Unicorn kisses?'

'Nuh-uh.' I'm barely keeping a straight face.

'*Mi corazón*, now you're just saying no for the sake of it.'

'Aren't I a pain in the arse?'

Rafael whirls me around in the middle of the lane between the stalls. Dizzy, I end up in his arms. 'You are *my* pain in the arse and I love you,' he says.

Then his lips meet mine and, I swear, this is real.

But as much as I want to melt into Rafael's kiss and stay there for the next few months, I can't concentrate knowing that Matt and Mabs are behind us. She's clearly on my ex's side. She's been chatting to him like they're long-lost friends. Worse, Martha is listening to their every word too.

This is *just* what we need. It's going to be hard enough pulling this off as it is. Now everyone seems happy to have Matt trailing along. I can't object without risking the real circumstances of our break-up coming out.

He doesn't know it, but Matt is holding my whole future to ransom.

Chapter 10

'Why didn't you mention about you and Mabs?' I ask Rafael a few days later as we walk together towards the reception venue. That's the venue that already has my (non-refundable at this late stage) deposit. 'Not that it matters,' I add. 'I was just wondering, that's all.'

I admit it's not the most eye-catching approach towards the filter house, down the A-road, unless one has a thing for 80s tower blocks. But wait till he sees the actual place I've booked. Even though it was raining when I first saw it, I fell in love. It's going to look spectacular in the summer sunshine.

I snap another pic. My readers really can't get enough of all this wedding planning. My likes and comments are going through the roof!

That's what I've got to keep reminding myself about. This is all for my future. I'm so close to being big enough to get sponsorship. Not just free stuff, but actual money. I can practically count the fees coming in already. #makealivinginmypyjamas. #lifegoals.

'Things are sometimes complicated with Mabs,' he tells me. 'Not because we're together or anything like that. We are much better friends than anything else.'

I'm starting to wonder whether she's come to the same conclusion. 'Does Mabs think so?'

Rafael pulls me so suddenly into his arms that I hardly have time to react. 'It doesn't matter, *mi corazón*, because it's you that I'm marrying.' He's giving me that look again. 'It's you that I love, you that has my heart, my soul, my life in your hands. It's you.'

'Erm, I . . . Oh, right, very good,' I say, giggling as I pull away. 'Don't wear yourself out before Martha gets here. But that was very good. Convincing.'

Sweat is starting to trickle down my neck and the weather isn't totally responsible. I always feel silly using the little battery fan that Rowan gave me last year, but it does work a treat for cooling hot commutes and, I hope, hot conversations.

'*Gracias*.' Then he catches sight of the old Victorian pumping station at the entrance to the reservoir. With its red-brick exterior and fancy turrets, it couldn't be called anything other than The Castle. 'You've booked a climbing centre for me!' he says. 'And you say the wedding's going to be no fun.'

'Yeah, I booked it because I'm just the type who'd pick the grown-up equivalent of a bouncy castle for my reception. And for the record, I have never said our wedding's going to be no fun.' He's grinning. 'Smart arse. Do you want me to abseil down a wall to dinner in my wedding dress? I'll pass, thanks. Come on, I promise this will be much better. It's not much to look at from the outside, but wait till you see inside.'

We continue past The Castle up the drive to the filter house. I had my doubts when I first saw it with Matt. Brutally rectangular and built in no-nonsense red brick, it screams functionality. But inside, oh my.

Martha is waiting for us out front with Photo Matt.

'You really haven't seen it before?' she asks Rafael. 'Hmm.'

I can hear the disbelief in her voice. Have we messed something up? She's tapping her pen on the top of her notebook. 'You haven't even given him a hint?'

Of course! A normal couple would have shared this kind of thing. But we're not normal, are we? We're frauds.

'I admire your restraint.' She's smiling at us. 'But of course, you two are the model of restraint. You know, before you told Matt.'

'Right.' I hope she can't hear the nervousness in my laugh.

She and Photo Matt follow us through the old oak double doors into the soaring space. Sunlight floods through the floor-to-ceiling cast-iron windows that run along the back of the building. And the ceiling is three floors high! The white iron girders, with their giant rivets, and great pipes running high above our heads add to the industrial feel.

I'm watching Rafael's face as he takes everything in: the old time-yellowed gauges set into the wall and the mysterious machine that looks like a Dalek and the iron ladder that runs all the way up the wall, beyond the pipes, to the ceiling.

He stops short when he sees the view. That was my reaction too. It is spectacular to look out past the deck at the back, down the weathered dock and over the large reservoir.

'I know, isn't it perfect?' I am beaming.

'Amazing. We could swim!' he says.

'No, we could not swim.' It's like he's never been to a wedding before.

'But the lake?'

'It's a reservoir and we are not swimming in London's water supply.'

Even though they do allow swimming and, I like to think, have a very good filtration system.

The view over the water is perfect. Definitely Instagram-worthy.

My photos show the sun glistening off the water with the brilliant blue sky as backdrop.

THIS IS IT, FRIENDS!!

I type into the caption on an especially pretty one.

The view before which Rafael and I will celebrate our marriage in less than two months! I can hardly believe it but all the plans are going perfectly. More later . . .

'What are you doing?' he asks, coming up behind me.

'Hmm? Just adding some hashtags.' And trying not to go weak at the knees because he's circled his arms around my waist and, if I lean back just a smidge, I can feel the heat of his chest through my shirt.

'Why not just enjoy the view instead of looking at it through your phone?' he asks. It's hard to miss the judgement.

'Because my followers want to see what we're doing.' He knows this.

'Not every second,' he mutters.

Even though I know it's the whole point, part of me wishes that Martha wasn't watching every move we're making. She's perfectly nice and all, but it would be much easier being ticked off in private.

'Look,' I say, holding the screen up. 'Forty likes already. This is why I'm doing this.'

'I know, *mi corazón*. This is business.' He lets go of my waist. I feel cold despite the summer's heat as I follow him back inside.

Just as I'm wrestling the wedding folder from my bag, the double doors squeak open. It was Rowan's idea to start collecting some of the looks I might like. I've ripped dozens of pages from magazines, scenes of romantic pink-and-white perfection hung with millions of fairy lights and strewn with flowers. It's fair to say I've got a theme in mind. I just need Rafael on board with it.

'God, not the wedding folder,' comes the deep voice from across the room.

My head snaps up. 'Matt! What are you doing here?'

'Mabs told me you were coming. Hi, Martha, nice to see you again.' He dazzles her with a killer smile. Of course she can't help but beam back. 'And Matt, hello,' he says to Photo Matt. 'Don't mind me. I thought I'd see how the wedding was coming along. Not that you're really getting married. Sorry, mate,' he adds for Rafael's benefit.

My face is flaming, but I *think* my voice stays under control. Which is more than I can say for my pulse. 'Matt, you are not welcome here. Please leave.'

'Well, technically, I'm still the groom as far as the venue knows. Or did you break the bad news to them already?'

I didn't. I will, though. 'You mean like I had to do with the registrar?'

That was so humiliating, having to make an appointment to cancel my marriage to Matt. It would have been easier if they hadn't been so nice about it. They had Kleenex at the ready and everything. Naturally I lost the plot as soon as I saw those.

'You only did that because you're marrying another bloke,' says Matt. 'Although I think we both know that's not really going to happen. Nelly, you can object all you like, but doesn't it mean something that you're even here?'

Does it? I admit nostalgia got hold of me the second I walked in. Matt and I had run around like little kids, pointing out all the amazing bits of the room. And when we saw that view! We sat on the end of the dock for a long time after the venue manager left us, imagining what our day would be like. It started with maybe having drinks outside first, if the weather was good. We wondered about having Chinese lanterns, then fireworks, and the ideas kept getting wilder until finally we were sailing to our venue at sunset on gondolas with everyone in eighteenth-century fancy dress.

But then Matt ended my dreams with an email. Also, incidentally, he broke my heart, though I can't mention that with Martha listening to every word.

'Why wouldn't I be here?' I say to Matt now. I will not let him see that I'm upset.

He rubs the pale stubble on his chin. I used to love that stubble, even when it felt rough on my face. Sometimes especially then. 'Think about it,' he says. 'This is our place. Why would you want to marry another bloke *here*? See? You don't. Which means you don't really want to marry him at all.'

'I'm not marrying him here,' I point out, though arguing over semantics sounds a bit off even to me. 'I'm receptioning with him here. And I'll tell you why. It's because I've already put a whopping great deposit down on it. Does that answer your question?'

He's got the nerve to shake his head. 'Anyway, I interrupted your discussion. Swimming, was it?'

'We're not swimming,' I say again.

Rafael crosses his arms. 'I get no say in my own wedding? Is there anything I *can* choose?'

'Welcome to my world,' says Matt. He gives Rafael a knowing look. Annoyingly, Rafael returns his look.

'Shut up.' Then to Rafael, 'Not you. We're choosing everything together.' This is going downhill fast. 'Sweetheart, other than this place, nothing is decided yet. We get to do all that together. I'm sorry if you didn't feel like that was the case.'

Instead of answering, Rafael takes me into his arms and suddenly we're twirling together around the bright room.

Wow, the man can dance! The way his arms support me, his hands gently pushing and pulling my body along with his, makes me feel like I'm flying across the floor. Rafael quietly croons 'The Way You Look Tonight' as we move together.

'I can't wait to dance with you at our wedding,' he says.

My answer is drowned out by Matt's slow clapping. As if he's got any right to be sarcastic. I didn't invite him to be here, did I?

'I see the ballroom dance lessons are going well,' he says. 'That looks very professional.'

Just as I nod, Rafael says, 'Nah, Latin music all the way.'

'Ballroom dance,' I say. 'You know, big band.'

'I hate big band. Unless it's a Latin band.'

'How can anyone hate big-band music?' I get all tappy-footed as soon as I hear those horns.

'It's old-man music,' says Rafael. 'It's what your grandmother would dance to.'

'Yes, right, and she will. At our wedding.'

As we stand glaring at each other, Matt clears his throat. 'Sorry, didn't mean to start a domestic.' He's smiling like he completely meant to start a domestic. 'Did you see the climbing centre on the way in?' he asks. 'That would be fun. Guests could have a go after dinner.'

When Rafael's face lights up I want to throw Matt into the reservoir. 'I'm all for having a fun wedding'—I choose to ignore Matt's snort—'but it is a wedding, not a company away day. So let's try to find compromises that we're both happy with.'

'Compromise all you like,' says Matt. 'It's not going to happen because Nelly loves me. And I love a big band, by the way. Now, Nelly, can we please talk? Alone?'

'No.'

'Shall we leave you?' Martha asks. Even I can see that she's only saying it for courtesy's sake. She's riveted to the spot.

'No, thank you, Martha. And no, Matt, I'm with Rafael now, so, dammit, we *are* getting married, and you'd better get used to the idea.'

He's quiet. Does that mean I've finally got through to him? I certainly hope so, because it's going to be very hard to sell my love story convincingly to Martha with my ex lurking around every corner.

'Then I'll just have to show you how devoted I am to you like this, with everyone around. That would be okay, Martha, wouldn't it?'

'Absolutely!' she says.

'Wait a second!' I sputter. 'You hate public displays of affection! You always have.'

Matt just shrugs, backing away towards the door. 'We'll just see about that, won't we?'

I round on Martha as soon as he's gone. 'He can't keep following us around like this. The story is supposed to be about me and Rafael.'

'But this is so much more romantic!' Martha says. 'Sorry, Nelly, but we've got the editorial control, remember? You agreed that we should reflect reality and not try to airbrush your life. This is *real*.'

Ha! I'd love to tell her that nothing about this situation is real. But I can't do that, can I?

Chapter 11

'But how can you hate that after hearing it?' I ask Rafael as we leave the jazz club together. 'You must have been listening to a different band. It's not rational.'

Soho is bustling with people enjoying the warm night. As I watch the other couples, I wonder whether Rafael and I look like them. Would anyone guess that he's only holding my hand because he's contractually obliged?

His warm grip tightens. '*Mi corazón*, disagreeing with you isn't irrational. Not like refusing to climb one little wall on your wedding day.'

He just won't drop the idea of watching me rappel down the side of a building with my wedding bouquet in my teeth. 'Guilty, then,' I say. 'I just can't see how anyone could be bored with so much happening on the stage. I loved it.'

'Even though it was too dark to take your pictures? Here's one for you: if a band plays in a nightclub and it's too dark to photograph them, did they make a sound?'

He can joke all he likes, but the lighting was a problem. This was another first that I've been teasing my readership about ever since Rafael admitted that he (irrationally) doesn't like big-band music. All my phone was able to catch were fuzzy red-tinged blurs. 'Wait a sec. I've got an idea. We have to go back.'

'What did you forget?'

'You'll see.' I lead him back to the club. 'Stand there.'

It's a bit yellow in the street light, but Rafael does make a nice subject standing below the club's sign. I snap half a dozen pics. 'Now point at the sign and I'll Boomerang you.'

'I have no idea what you're talking about.'

'Just point.'

He lifts his finger about two inches.

'Not like that. Point like you mean it.'

Rafael gestures like a game show host. 'Perfect. See?' I replay the video clip of him pointing and rewinding, pointing and rewinding.

'That looks ridiculous. People can't like that sort of thing.'

'They love it,' I tell him, adding hashtags. 'Stick with me, my friend, I'll make you a star.'

'Stick with me,' he says, grasping my hand again, 'and you'll hear some proper dance music.'

'I do know proper dance music,' I tell him. 'I'll have you know that I even know Colombian dance music.'

'Don't say Shakira,' he says, just as I say Shakira. 'That's just pop. This is proper Latin music.' To make his point, Rafael does a little step right there on the Soho street. I'm not saying it's sexy. I'm just saying that hips don't lie.

The music blares into the street from the open doorway he leads me to around the corner. 'I hear horns. We had horns back there at the jazz club. Just saying.'

'This isn't your old-man music. *I'm* just saying.'

A blanket of humidity settles over us as we descend the dark stairs. This doesn't seem to be any better for taking pictures.

Rafael opens the black door and even more sound rushes out at us. The cavernous room is heaving with writhing bodies. I've never seen so much hip action with my clothes on.

Rafael is already moving to the music. 'Come, let's dance.'

'You're kidding, right? I'm British.'

He just laughs as he pulls me into the mêlée. 'I'll show you,' he shouts in my ear. 'Listen to the beat. Hear it?'

I hear it. That doesn't mean I can dance to it. Everyone around me seems to be double-jointed. My joints are decidedly single. 'I can't.'

'You can. Everyone can. You just need to let yourself go.' He puts his palms on my hips. 'Like this. Gently.' I can feel his warm hands through my jeans as he slowly guides my hips to move with his. His face is beside my ear as we sway to the music. 'Nice? Just feel it.'

I'm definitely feeling something, but I'm not sure it's the music. 'Does this work on your dates?'

'Sometimes.' He laughs. 'Is it working on you?'

'Is it meant to?' Luckily the music drowns out the wobble in my voice.

'That depends.'

Just then, the tempo changes. Rafael grabs one hand and pushes my hips away with the other, spinning me around. As soon as I'm facing him again, he clasps me to him. 'Woah.'

'Dizzy?'

'Erm, yeah.' Let's go with dizzy. I can hardly breathe.

The band on stage moves from one song to the next, but I hardly notice the change. I'm too busy trying not to proposition Rafael every time he pulls another hip swivel on me. If English boys were this smooth, I'd probably be a mother of six by now.

By the time the band takes its break, I'm dripping with sweat. 'Drink?' Rafael asks.

'I could down an entire bucket of water.' Actually, I need it dumped over my head, because I've got to get over myself. We are *not* on a date. Just because we're moving together like extras in a porn film doesn't mean anything. This is all an act. I glance around me. Everyone here is dancing the same way. It must be what South Americans do. I can't let myself get carried away by some illusion.

It is definitely all an act.

I mean, he's probably still dating other women. He was having sleepovers just a few weeks ago. Or at least dinner-overs, and we all know where that sometimes leads. Those aren't the actions of a committed man. And why am I even thinking about this, anyway, when I'm barely out of a relationship?

That's it! I'm on the rebound. That's why these feelings are bubbling over. Remember Jenny's over/under theory? That's all this is, so you can calm down, butterflies. Back in your cocoons, or wherever you go, because I am not falling for Rafael. And you can forget about making me feel giddy every time I lay eyes on him. Tell the little heaters that keep turning on whenever he looks at me to unplug themselves too.

Rafael's question breaks into my stern talking-to. 'So? Good, yes?'

'Very good,' I say. 'I guess this is why Colombian women are all fit and gorgeous.' He's smiling at me. 'Because they lose buckets in water weight whenever they go dancing.' He's still smiling. 'Not that I know any Colombians other than Mabs, so maybe she's not a fair sample. But she is fit. And gorgeous. I guess she dances?'

I beg you, mouth, please stop talking.

'She dances,' he says, sending me into visions of them swivel-hipping together. The thought makes me feel a little queasy.

'Have you taken her here?' I regret the question as soon as I ask it.

'Does it matter?' He sips his drink. 'Let's talk about something else.'

Why? Because he doesn't want to tell me about Mabs? 'Okay, sure.'

'Wouldn't music like this be more fun at our party?' he says.

'Can you imagine my parents trying to dance to this? My gran would break a hip. It's not practical.'

'Are you always practical?'

'I try to be. Otherwise things go wrong. Well, they go wrong anyway, but at least if I plan, there's slightly more chance of not fucking up.'

Rafael frowns. 'Nelly, why do you put yourself down? You're always saying that you fuck up, but who tells you this? Whoever it is, you shouldn't listen.'

'Oh, but it's a fact,' I say. 'Nothing works out the way I think it's going to. It never has, really. That's why . . . It's why having Matt break up with me was so bad. Because this time I was really sure everything would go right. I was wrong. Again.'

Rafael takes my hands into his. 'Has it ever occurred to you that things have gone right? Maybe *this* is the right thing.'

His deep brown eyes are so dark as they stare into mine. I couldn't look away if I wanted to. I don't ever want to look away. 'Maybe,' I whisper.

'You're not meant to be with Matt,' he goes on, like he's reading my mind. 'Some part of you must know that, even if you're grieving now. You're meant for better things. A better man.'

I could be wrong but his lips definitely seem closer to mine than they were a second ago. We stare at each other as the people around us jostle for bar space. A digger couldn't dislodge me from this spot right now.

Rafael leans in until his lips are inches from me. 'You'll find him,' he whispers into my ear.

Right. This is a pep talk. Like, between friends. What else would it be? We've known each other for about two minutes. Must regain my composure. 'Right, of course,' I say.

The trouble is, I think I've already found him. Despite knowing that this is nothing more than a business transaction. Even though I'm still smarting from the mother of all relationship burns. I can't explain why I feel like this. It makes no sense. I know it's not rational. It's far from practical, when Rafael doesn't feel the same way.

But there you go.

#Hopelesslyinlove.

PART 2

TO LOVE AND TO CHERISH

Chapter 12

The last thing I planned on when I schemed up this little idea was to fall in love. Or in deep-like or whatever this is. I can't believe I'm even saying that. What is wrong with me? I was engaged to be married to another bloke. Engaged! As in, in a relationship in which I thought I wanted to spend the rest of my life. So how on earth did this happen?

It can't all be a rebound thing. Not even Michael Jordan had that kind of game. I'm starting to wonder whether maybe what I felt for Matt had a smidge of wishful thinking about it. If I'm honest with myself, I wasn't always sure how I felt about him, but whenever he had the nerve to have the same questions about me, I was suddenly certain he was the love of my life. Then I was grateful for whatever romantic gestures he did make, no matter how unintended or, now that I think about it, insufficient. Sort of like when you get completely carried away and tell a dog he's a good boy a million times just because he manages not to crap on the kitchen floor.

What I mistook for love was actually thankfulness for Matt not fouling my heart.

I sneak a glance at Rafael as we wedge ourselves into the Tube carriage with the other commuters. It's packed, and stifling, with post-work deodorant breakdowns left, right, and centre. I only hope that the man pressing up against my back is holding a briefcase. Otherwise I'm ringing the police as soon as we get above ground. He backs up a few millimetres when I give him a pointedly dirty look over my shoulder. It doesn't help. #stillcloseenoughtoreadmythoughts.

This is exactly why I usually take the bus. At least there's a waft of fresh air with its windows open, even if I have to stand then too.

I'd be on that bus now, creeping in the rush-hour traffic towards my meal-for-one, if Rafael hadn't rung.

I nearly fell out of my office chair when he asked me to have dinner with him tonight. Just like that, out of the blue, and not because Martha wants to film, either. She won't even be there.

I'm not one to count my snogs before they happen, but this feels like our first proper date. Whatever Mr Space Invader behind me is poking into my thigh, I'll put up with it for this chance.

'Why won't you tell me where we're going?' I ask Rafael.

'Because then it's not a surprise,' he says. 'It's a restaurant.'

'Yeah, I guessed that when you said it was dinner. Is it Italian?'

'I'm not telling you.'

'French? Spanish? Something South American? Colombian?'

'Still not telling.'

'Not seafood?'

'Why don't you just wait and see?'

'Because I like to anticipate. Or not, in the case of seafood.'

'Anticipate a good meal.'

'Will this meal involve . . . pasta?'

'Give up,' he says.

There's a horrific screech as the train rounds a corner. Proper ear-splitting stuff that makes a few of the passengers wince.

As we stand squashed together, Rafael's fingers find the spot on my neck that gives me shivers.

It always made me ticklish when Matt did that. It's not ticklishness that I'm feeling now.

'You never know where Martha is,' he says, glancing back through the window between the carriages. 'She could pop up from anywhere.'

'She does have a knack for that.'

On the one hand, I love that he's always willing to stay in character. On the other, this is very confusing.

Then Rafael takes a deep breath. 'Nelly, may I ask you something? Are you questioning what we're doing? *Why* we're doing it?'

Oh, no, he's having second thoughts. I bet it's because

Matt's turned back up, like a bad, fiancée-rejecting penny who ruins everything. 'Are you worried about Matt?'

His fingers stop their stroking. 'It's not ideal that he's back on the scene,' he answers. 'Unless you want him here.'

'I don't want him here.'

'Good, I don't either,' he says.

'He's just complicating things.'

'I'm relieved to hear you say that.'

'I mean, Martha loves it, naturally,' I go on, 'but this is supposed to be about us. Not us. I mean about the wedding. For the feature.'

'Then you don't feel—'

His words are drowned out as the train screeches around another corner. God, that's deafening. I'm left lip-reading (not easy – who knew that lips have accents?). He's uncomfortable with what we're doing. I understand that, but he's the one with the most to gain from this. Yes, it's the publicity for me, but this is his only chance to keep everything that he's built here: all his friends and his career, not to mention the kids he loves coaching.

I can't stop him from backing out, obviously, if he really wants to. The best I can do is assure him that it's still a good idea.

Emphatically, I shake my head. 'Not a bit. And you shouldn't either.'

His eyes search mine. 'If you're sure. I shouldn't have said anything.'

He must assume that Martha isn't clinging to the outside

of the carriage, because he drops his hand from my neck. I'm imagining that I can still feel it, though.

People jostle past us as the Tube doors open at the next station. 'I've never been surer of anything, Rafael. Really. We're only doing what we have to.'

We don't touch for the rest of the journey.

The covered market where he leads me is tucked around the back of Brixton station. Even now after work, the summer light streams through the Victorian arched glass ceiling, brightening the avenue between the shops. Most have tables in front, or stacks of wares: richly decorated woven baskets, bright frocks, tall buckets full of fragrant flowers and fresh fruit and veg piled in colourful crates.

'This is it,' says Rafael, stopping in front of the restaurant. People sit at each of the half-dozen small tables outside. Inside is nearly as full. I wouldn't call it atmospheric in the romantic sense – the overhead lighting is too bright for that – but it definitely looks authentic. Ha, listen to me. Like I would know authentic Colombian if I fell over it. It's very casual, anyway, with wooden tables and chairs, a stone-tiled floor, dark panelling halfway up the walls and faux brick on the bar at the back that separates the diners from the tiny kitchen. There are enough straw hats and cowboy kitsch dotted around to hint at the countryside.

'I guessed Colombian!' I tell him. 'You said no.'

'Did not. I didn't answer you. That's different.' His hand on the small of my back is practically burning as he follows me to the little tucked-away table. Meanwhile, he's chatting amiably in his own language with the waitress who's in front of me.

'I'm the meat in a Spanish sandwich!' I tell him once we're seated. 'You, me and the waitress.' Then I worry that that sounds like I'm suggesting a threesome. 'What's Spanish for meat?'

'*Carne*,' he says, expertly rolling the 'r' on his tongue, which only makes me think about his expert tongue.

'I like hearing you speak Spanish. I don't know why I expected English from you when this is your native language.'

'Ha! Is this where I admit that I've been faking all this time? That I am really Jamie from Essex?'

His pronunciation (Haymie) makes me laugh. 'You're definitely not giving off a Haymie-from-Essex vibe. No, I'm just used to you in English, that's all. I like the Spanish.'

Rafael considers me for a moment. 'I felt the same way seeing you at your parents. You seemed different. More at home. Even if you are the only person from Cornwall who won't eat seafood.'

He's got his long legs extended on either side of mine under the table. We're barely touching, but I'm very aware of him. 'I'm not a freak just because I won't eat oysters,' I say. 'It's not like I'm rejecting crisps or toast soldiers or anything.'

'Or turkey twizzlers. The height of British cuisine. How do you twizzle a turkey?'

'That's an over-eighteen conversation.'

'We're over eighteen.' He reaches across the table for my hand.

How am I supposed to remember that this is all fake when he stares at me like that? 'You don't have to do this, you know. When Martha isn't here, I mean.' But I don't move my hand. His grip is so warm and reassuring.

When he sits back, the broken contact makes me want to cry. 'It's nice to stay in character, no? Unless you mind.'

'I don't mind.' I'm suddenly finding the menu *very* interesting. Maybe trying to sound out all the unfamiliar words will calm my heart. I need a distraction.

Then I remember something. I take a small package from my handbag. 'These came for you.'

He looks inside. Then his eyes meet mine. 'You are joking.'

'Well, no. The brand sent them. I think they're nice, don't you?'

He pulls out a handful of bow ties. Admittedly, they are a bit bright in this overhead light. 'So you want to marry a 1950s gentleman from the American South? Have I got time to grow a handlebar moustache?'

'They're not old-fashioned! They're super trendy.'

'Maybe on Instagram. You do know that's not real, right?'

I pick up a pink and purple one. 'This is a really good brand.'

'Of bow tie,' he says. 'A really good brand *of bow tie*. Listen to what you're saying.'

'You don't have to wear one if you really don't want to. I just thought that it could liven up one of your work suits. That way you won't have to spend money on a new one. It *is* only for one day and you're already spending a lot.'

'But I want to look pretty on my special day.' He bats his eyelashes at me. 'You can come with me to pick one out if you want. Girls love to shop.'

'Don't be sexist. As if I'd want to stand around watching you try on clothes.' Listen to me. All bluster. I'd happily go with him to have his MOT done. 'I'm just saying that one of your work suits would be fine. What are you thinking of, suitwise?'

'Definitely something summery,' he says. 'Maybe pale blue or green, or orange? I like orange and yellow.'

I'm sorry I mentioned the bow ties now. He's going to look like a parakeet.

'I want to stand out on my wedding day too,' he says.

There's standing out and then there's standing out. 'I'm really thinking one of your work suits would be fine.'

'Are you wearing one of your old dresses?' he asks. 'You could, you know, and save some money.'

'You're hilarious.'

Our banter stops briefly when the waitress comes to take our order. 'May I?' He gestures to the menu. 'There is a lot that I'd love you to try.'

'Be my guest.' I couldn't pronounce anything anyway.

Rafael starts rattling off dishes. Every time I think he's

finished, he glances again and adds something else. The waitress nods without writing down a thing.

'A wedding dress is completely different,' I continue once the waitress leaves. 'Nobody has a wedding dress lying around, unless you're Miss Havisham.' Inwardly I wince, because I nearly was. If I'd been a bit more on the ball before Matt pulled the plug, or Rafael and I hadn't hatched this plan, I'd now be the owner of one unused wedding dress. I could have worn it every time I ate my Thai delivery alone.

'Will they mind if I get a few pics in here?' I ask. I've already got my phone out.

'Go ahead. You've got a job to do.'

Something in the way he says that makes me pause. 'It is for work, you know. I don't do this for fun.'

'You like it, though.'

'Well, yes, obviously. Otherwise I wouldn't be trying to make a living from it. But it's still work. I don't always want to be thinking about the next post, about the right angle for photos. I can't pass by anything without seeing it as having potential for my account. It's not always fun, you know.'

'I'm sorry, *mi corazón*, I do understand. Go take your photos.'

Outside, the evening sun bathes the front of the restaurant in golden-hour light. It's hard to take a bad pic at this time of day. Still, I need to get the right angle and composition. That was one of the hardest things to learn. I never consciously knew why some people's photos were so appealing, until I started reading up on it. It turned out that I was doing it all wrong, bunging snaps up every time I thought they looked nice. Now I know better.

Walking back along the market, checking my screen every few feet, the vantage point starts to come together. The cheery yellow-painted iron trusses high above, the colourful flags hanging down, the red and white striped butcher's awning further down and the variety of shop signs lining the bustling avenue, the colourful wares displayed in perfectly Instagrammable heaps outside the shops.

And Mabs.

Mabs is standing in the middle of the avenue, gazing at me through my phone screen. Even the golden-hour light can't diffuse her expression.

The feeling is mutual. 'What are you doing here?' I ask. What I really want to know is, how she can look even more intimidatingly gorgeous than she did at the dress shop? She's only wearing jeans and a white shirt, with perfectly average ballerina flats. Granted, her big slouchy pebbled leather bag is obviously designer, but so is mine, and it never looks as good on me.

It must be the way she doesn't seem to have made an ounce of effort. Her make-up is barely there – her tan does all the work – though she might have on some tinted lip gloss. I only say that because I still don't believe that colour pink is natural.

'Rafael invited me. The same as you, I assume.' Her blonde highlights shimmer in her also-blonde hair. People stare at her as they pass us.

'See you when you finish your pics.' She starts for the restaurant's door.

I still haven't got quite the right shot. 'I'm finished,' I say, following her.

As we go back inside, I catch her side-eying me. I catch her because I'm side-eying her.

'Mi cariño!' Mabs throws herself into Rafael's arms. You'd think he's just rescued her from a deserted island. Then she launches into rapid-fire Spanish, which I'm sure she's only doing because she knows I can't understand her.

But Rafael notices. 'English, Mabs,' he says. 'We don't want to leave Nelly out. I thought I'd get you two together since, well, so that you can be friends.'

I wonder if he catches the slight curve of her lip. And she's definitely wearing gloss. 'Of course. I'm just so excited. How long has it been?'

Puhlease. I know for a fact that they saw each other at the weekend.

'A few years anyway,' he says and I understand that this is another of their haunts. I should have known. 'The menu is the same.'

'Please order what I like,' says Mabs, finally taking off her super glam sunglasses. 'You know what I like, *cariño*. Are there no cameras tonight? I'm surprised.'

'No, it's just us,' Rafael says. He can't really be oblivious to her attitude.

'Like the old days.' She glances at me. 'Almost.'

I could make my excuses and leave them to reminisce, but

since Mabs would just love that, a five-alarm fire wouldn't get me out of here now. 'I know it's a bit awkward having the magazine around all the time,' I say, 'but it's a small price to pay to marry the love of my life.' I reach for Rafael's hand.

Ha! There it is. Mabs might be ultra-poised, but the hurt skitters across her expression.

She does love Rafael. I knew I was right.

My triumph is fleeting, though, before she's back on form. 'And were you paid a big price?' she asks. 'Selling yourself . . . your wedding, I mean?'

Rafael cuts off my answer, which is a shame because it could have sliced through concrete. 'I admire the way Nelly is building up her profile. She's very dedicated.'

'I'm sure.'

Again, he ignores her tone. Instead, he's looking at me with pure adoration. I could happily snuggle into that look for the next few decades or so. 'I could never do all that Nelly does.'

This is news to me, especially given his tepid reaction when I wanted to take a few snaps before.

'But you have got to do it now, no?' Mabs asks. 'Because you're half of the wedding show.' *Show*. She doesn't even bother to try hiding the sneer.

'I don't mind being in the photos,' he tells her. 'Nelly's the one making all the effort. Honestly, it's like having two jobs. I had no idea what was involved.' Then he turns to me. 'Mabs is on Instagram too.'

'Oh?' I say, just because he's staring at me like he

expects us to bond now over that. I bet her feed is full of pouty lip pics and mad nights out. Boorring. 'What's your username?'

The waitress starts unloading a huge tray of dishes while we follow each other's accounts. Scrolling through her feed – which are all of blurry Mabs in another dark club or pub or restaurant – I can't help but notice that she's getting hundreds of likes. There's no way those are all real. She must be buying them. '*Cariño*, all my favourites!' Mabs cries. 'You've read my mind as usual.' Then she aims her phone at me. Obediently, I smile for her, now that we're Insta-besties and all.

'I wanted you to try all the food I love,' Rafael says. But he's talking to me, not her. 'I hope you like it as much as poached salmon.' We share a smile.

'I've never understood why the English boil everything to death,' Mabs says, helping herself to tiny scoops from each dish. Then she cuts a little pastry in half. It's barely a mouthful! She's definitely the type who'll eat a thimbleful and declare herself stuffed. Then she'll say she's fat just so everyone can tell her she's not.

I'm a big enough person to ignore her jibe at my country's entire cuisine. I just wonder why she's got to ruin the night when Rafael and I were having a perfectly nice time without her.

Rafael holds out his fork to me. 'Try.'

Without even asking what it is, I open up. 'Mmm, delicious!' Savoury, creamy and meaty.

He pops a forkful into his own mouth. 'Tamale,' he says. 'Corn dough.'

'I could eat like this all the time,' I tell him.

'You couldn't,' says Mabs, pushing morsels around her plate. 'You'd get fat.'

'Mmm, fat and happy!' I say. 'Thank you, Rafael, for sharing this with me.'

'Well, you shared Cornwall,' he says. 'And your family. I only wish mine could meet you before the wedding.'

'Your mother hasn't met Nelly?' Mabs asks. 'I'm surprised she's letting you get married without her approval.'

For once Mabs is quiet as Rafael lets loose in Spanish. 'She will love Nelly as much as I do,' he finishes in English.

Mabs couldn't look more pleased with herself. She knows she's got one over on me now. Well, I won't let that stand. I can hardly believe I'm about to do this, but sod it. 'What do you think about going away for the weekend?' I ask Rafael, as if Mabs isn't even there. 'Remember, I'm signed up for bargains at those stately homes?' He nods, playing his part. This is just the sort of thing that real couples would know about each other. 'Well, one came through today that includes all the meals. It's supposed to be divine. We *have* been saying we should take a minibreak, what with all the wedding stuff going on.' I know. I'm pushing my luck with that last bit, but it does sound very real, doesn't it?

Rafael's eyes bore deeply into mine. '*Mi corazón*, that sounds like heaven. Please book it for us.'

Chapter 13

People make it sound like butterflies are these gentle, fluttery creatures. Clearly they've never met the ones in my tummy, because they feel about as delicate as a flock of albatrosses flapping to take off. Rafael is oblivious to my albatrosses, though. He's too busy singing Colombian rap and pretending he's Lewis Hamilton on the motorway.

'How can you know all the words to every single song?' I ask as he downshifts the car off the exit. 'Obviously that's the sign of a misspent youth.'

'The same way you know the words to all the ABBA songs.' He glances at me with a smile. 'Am I right?'

'Guilty.' Then another song comes on. 'Hey, I know this one, "Hips Don't Lie"! I never pegged you as a Shakira fan.' I'm sure my seat-wriggling is super-impressive.

Rafael deftly sways in the driver's seat as he purrs the words. 'She's a hometown girl,' he says.

'Not exactly your average girl next door,' I say, picturing the bombshell blonde.

'Yeah, she's cute,' he says.

Cute? Puppies and baby bunnies are cute. Egg cups with

panda faces are cute. Shakira looks like . . . like . . . Why haven't I noticed before? Shakira looks like Mabs.

The hotel comes into view around the bend of the long drive. Its deep green lawns roll off into the distance all around it, dotted with riotous formal flower beds and hedges that look like they've been trimmed with nail scissors.

'This is something,' says Rafael. He manoeuvres the car into a parking space beside the building.

So far, so perfect. The minute I opened the email with this deal, I started having fantasies about a dirty weekend away. I hope they've given us the four-poster room like I asked.

'Thanks for giving up your coaching this weekend to do this,' I say.

'It's okay. This was important. Besides, the other guys are happy to fill in.' He points to the building as we're carrying our weekend bags towards the front door. 'Do you do this a lot? This stately home thing?'

'God, no. It's only because there was a deal and I can Instagram the whole thing.' I don't mention my other reason, naturally. 'I'm usually a little lower-key than this.'

He takes my bag from me and slings it over his shoulder. 'Like camping?'

I point upwards. 'Higher-key than that. I assume you mean camping in a tent.'

'How about a campervan?'

'I'm not sure. Is there a proper loo in this campervan?' The gravel drive crunches under our feet.

'For the sake of the conversation, let's say yes.'

'Maybe for a night or two. I think I really prefer sleeping in permanent structures. I take it you like to camp?'

'Love it. Maybe we'll go sometime.'

I knew this weekend was a good idea! I'm practically floating when he holds open the front door for me.

Then I see inside.

We both come back down to reality with a bump.

It might look like *Downton Abbey* out front, but this is a different programme altogether. Much more *Homes Under the Hammer* (the derelict special). Two of the windows are boarded up from the inside. What little light there is comes from a few industrial builder's bulbs strung clumsily on yellow cable over the reception desk. It looks like there was a fire near one corner, judging from the blackened wall above a blown-out socket. The paint on the other walls is chipped and scratched.

'Doing some renovations?' Rafael asks the young woman behind the desk.

More like demolition.

'Constantly,' she says. She is dressed all in black, with her light hair pinned neatly back. She giggles as she stares at him. I don't blame her. He's definitely the most attractive feature in this room, by a long stretch. Cardboard boxes have been flattened and gaffer-taped all over the floor. The curtain rails are bare. Where the wall isn't burnt, its plaster is stained and flaking.

It could be shabby chic if there was anything chic about it.

'I requested a special room,' I told her. 'They said they couldn't guarantee it, but I should ask when we check in.'

The girl taps something into her computer. 'The Anne Boleyn room, yes, it's available. With the four-poster bed.' She smirks at us both.

'It'll be good for pics,' I explain to Rafael.

'Right, pics,' he says, while I take the two sets of keys from the receptionist.

Upstairs, the hall is dimly lit too, by ancient-looking wall sconces this time. But bright sunlight pours over the threshold when I open the door to our room.

The tall windows look as old as the house, but there's a second set of insulating modern panes on the inside. Both sets are open on the bottom, though, and the warm breeze gently wafts the curtains.

I admit I was starting to lose hope in this weekend, but the room really does look like the photos online. Rectangles of sunlight illuminate the golden-hued carpet, which matches the silky-looking bedding on the four-poster. The desk and chair might be a little banged up, but it is an old hotel. That makes the furniture authentic, not banged up.

'Do you have any drawer preference?' Rafael asks.

I wasn't planning to unpack. We're only here for one night. 'No, you go ahead. Sorry about downstairs. It's not quite up to the marketing in the email they sent, but this is nice, isn't it? You'd think they'd mention something like a total renovation happening.'

'That's probably why it was a deal. They wouldn't get anyone paying full price for a building site, especially if they admitted it before people arrived.'

I pull my swimsuit from my bag. 'At least there's the indoor pool.'

'And chocolates on our pillows,' he says, throwing me one.

'Don't eat that!' He freezes with the chocolate halfway to his mouth.

'Why, do you think it might be poisoned?'

'Wrap it back up, please. I need to photograph the bed before we mess everything up.' I grab a few of the fluffy towels from the bathroom and arrange the stack on the bed. Then I drape my suit on top.

It only takes a few seconds to get the photos I want. Once the best one posts (#romanceoverload), I scan my feed.

Mabs has posted a photo of me, and not a flattering one, either. I've got my mouth wide open with an empanada stuffed in. Charming.

Rafael's new "fiancée", Mabs has captioned it.

What are those quotes supposed to mean? I hope it's a translation error. We haven't done anything to raise her suspicion. Have we?

'Thanks, I'm done,' I tell Rafael. 'The chocolate is all yours.' Picking up my own, I throw myself onto the bed. 'Oof!' The impact knocks the chocolate from my hand, not to mention my breath from my lungs. 'Crikey,' I gasp. 'Is there even a mattress on here?'

Rafael lifts the cover. 'I guess it's not quite soft enough?'

He sits much more carefully on the mattress. 'I see what you mean.'

This is going to be like sleeping on a dining table. 'Some Anne Boleyn suite. No wonder people didn't live past their forties in her day. Forget the plague, they probably died of back problems.' I grab my swimsuit. 'Want a swim before dinner?'

'Maybe they'll let us sleep on their sunloungers,' he says. 'Think we can smuggle two back up here?'

Chapter 14

We can hear the pool activity before we find it. Echoey children's shouts ping towards us as we turn down another hallway. 'I'm guessing it's this way,' Rafael says. His linen shirt is unbuttoned over his swim trunks and his flip-flops are so ancient that the acid-green straps are faded. That man was born to be on a beach.

'That's a lot of noise for only a few kids,' he says as we let ourselves into the huge conservatory through the heavy glass door. I count three kids in the pool and one littler one on a chair with two adults. The whole pool deck area is covered in green outdoor carpeting.

Towels are stacked by the door. 'How about over there?' I ask, grabbing two towels. In other words, as far from the children as possible without sitting in the car park.

I can feel a trickle of sweat race between my shoulder blades. That water is going to feel so good. Carefully spreading the towel over one of the sunloungers, I kick off my sandals to sit on the chair. 'Ahh, perfect.' Even though it is incredibly muggy in here. It must be from the sun that's beating through the steamed-up window panes. It's evaporating the pool water. In fact, I'm sure I hear dripping. I bet this is what the rainforest is like. We've got our own little ecosystem in here.

Rafael peels off his shirt. I'm trying not to look, I really am. But if I *were* to look, it would only be to note his perfectly tanned six-pack and just the right (in other words, sexy) amount of hair on his chest without tipping him into missing-link territory.

Then I note something else. Not on Rafael, thank goodness, but on the floor behind him. From this angle, something seems to be sprouting from the carpet. Not all over. Just near the edges of the windows. 'Are those mushrooms?' I ask Rafael. 'There, in the corner.'

He squints. 'Looks like it. Maybe they're magic.'

'Maybe they're dirty.' Just how much organic matter must there be in a carpet before it can grow mushrooms? More than I'd like to walk on in bare feet, I'm guessing.

Rafael swings his long legs off the lounger. 'Swim?' He's standing on that carpet without flip-flops.

'Did you not just see those mushrooms?' With my phone angled just right, the pool picture I capture does look inviting. I can always check it later and airbrush out any fungus.

'But I'm not walking near the mushrooms,' Rafael points out. 'And before you ask, smell that chlorine. It's got to be clean, no?'

No, not necessarily. Common sense is telling me there's probably all kinds of funkiness in that water, but my desire to get into the pool with Rafael tells my common sense to pipe down with its killjoy opinions.

I'm not going in there barefooted, though. If they don't clean the deck, what are the chances they bother with the bottom of the pool? I follow him into the warm water with my flip-flops on.

The problem is that my feet keep slipping off the rubber. It must be the water reacting with all the moisturiser I've slathered on.

Meanwhile, Rafael's long strokes pull him easily through the water. After every few laps he stops at one end, looks at me, grins and kicks off again. Watching him exercise isn't the romantically sexy start I'd hoped for, but I've got no chance of swimming with these shoes on. In fact, I feel a bit foolish now.

'This is so relaxing,' he says, once he's finished his breaststroke training. 'Thanks again for booking.' Then, with a toothy smile, he shakes the water off his hair and, I swear, he's the most gorgeous bloke I've ever seen in real life. I mean pant squirmingly hot. I'd have booked us into the Ritz to be with him right now.

'Too bad Martha's not here,' he goes on. 'She'd love seeing this.'

'Seeing what?' I'm hardly breathing.

He moves behind me and loops his arms loosely around my waist. My head finds the hollow under his collarbone as he gently floats backwards. 'This,' he says into my ear. I can feel his breath on my bare shoulder.

'It's not bad,' I murmur. Then I stop myself from saying anything that might break this spell.

We drift around the pool like that. Rafael must have a foot on the bottom so we don't go under. His slow, deep breaths gently press his chest against my back. The wet hair on his torso is soft and ticklish.

But not everyone around the pool is on mute. ''Scuse me, your phone's ringing.' The boy who was sitting with his parents is carrying my phone to the pool's edge. I'm sure he's just trying to be helpful, but iPhones and pools don't go together very well.

'Sorry,' I tell Rafael, making a wake behind me as I rush to the edge of the pool before the boy drops it in. 'Oh.' Matt's timing is great as always. 'What do you want?' I bark into the phone.

'You sound like you're in the loo,' he says. 'Echoey.'

'I'm at the pool. Not that it's any of your business. You're ringing because . . .?'

'Just to talk. What pool?'

'We're at a luxury spa hotel, actually. Rafael and I.' I don't mention the mushrooms. Let him imagine we're at Buckingham Palace. If the Queen ran a spa for commoners.

'Yet you answered,' he says. 'If you were with me, you wouldn't have wanted to answer your phone. Especially to talk to another man.' He couldn't sound smugger. 'Obviously Mr Salsa there isn't doing it for you. He must hate that you're talking to me right now.'

'Rafael is secure enough not to worry about me taking

a call from my *ex*,' I say pointedly. 'Now did you ring for a reason or was it just to bother me?'

'No special reason, just to say that I love you.'

'Goodbye, Matt.'

'Go back to Mr Salsa. He's probably getting worried.'

'I doubt that.' But Rafael is already climbing out of the pool. Thanks very much, Matt. 'I've got to go or we'll be late for our dinner. It's going to be very romantic.'

'Don't let me get in your way,' he says as I watch Rafael towel off beside our chairs.

'I don't intend to.' I hang up on him.

'Sorry, it was just Matt bothering me,' I tell Rafael as he takes the phone from me so that I can climb up the ladder. I don't know why I say this, when he heard the whole conversation. I talk too much when I'm nervous.

He holds out my towel so I can dry off. 'That's okay, Nelly, you have a life too.'

'But not with Matt. He's not part of my life.' *Not like you are*, I want to say. Instead, I concentrate on unsticking my dress from my wet swimsuit. There's no reason to lounge here anyway. It would take weeks to air-dry in this humidity.

'Do you want to sit for a bit or . . .?'

'I'm happy going upstairs,' he says, and we make our way to the exit.

'*Mi corazón*, it's fine,' Rafael continues as we walk. 'You can't expect him to give up easily. Not when you had everything you had together. I know I wouldn't. In his place.'

'Yeah, well, you wouldn't be in his place because you'd

never have dumped me like he did.' That came out a little angrier than I meant it to. 'I mean, I don't mean that I'm so great that you'd— That I . . . I mean you're nicer than that.'

That's true. Now I realise that. Matt wasn't always the perfect partner.

Sometimes he really threw me off-kilter, especially when he got into a mood. Maybe because there was too much at stake. I suspect that I did give in a lot for the sake of our relationship. Not usually on important things, though, to be honest, I was pretty good at avoiding prickly topics with him. Looking back now, that's a rather uncomfortable thought. He didn't always seem as worried about keeping me happy. 'You're nicer than Matt,' I say again.

We're standing in front of our door. He takes a step closer. 'I would never have done what he did.'

'That's because you're a decent human being who wouldn't run off to party at the beach just because you're afraid to make a commitment.' Oops, there's that anger again.

'It's because . . . yes,' he says. 'And because you're a remarkable person. You run yourself down a lot, and you really shouldn't. Not that I'm telling you what to do. I just don't want you to forget that you're actually pretty great.'

'That's nice of you to say,' I tell him. 'Thank you.'

'That's what fiancés are for.'

I laugh when I recall that I said the very same thing to him when we were on our way to see my parents. 'Even fake ones.'

But he doesn't carry on the joke. 'Right.' He turns from me to unlock the room door. 'Do you mind if I shower first?'

It seems that my pep talk is finished. 'Go ahead. I'll take some more photos. This room really is Instagram perfect.'

'That's what we're here for,' he says, before the bathroom door clicks closed.

By the time we reach our table, my tummy is rumbling like crazy. Getting ready takes way longer when you're trying courteously not to see each other naked. At least the builders haven't turned the dining room upside down. It's lit almost completely with candles standing on crisp white linen and in candelabras on sideboards dotted around the walls. The glasses and cutlery glisten in the soft light.

Rafael pulls out my chair for me. 'Thank you, sir . . . Sorry,' I add when my tummy rumbles again. There's definitely a protest being organised in there. 'I haven't eaten since breakfast, and then I only had the last bit of leftover curry. I'm really looking forward to this.' The dinner is included with the room, and I'm planning to make a pig of myself. One should never seduce on an empty stomach.

'You look pretty tonight,' says Rafael. 'I like'—he zigzags his finger at me—'that kind of top.'

I know I'm blushing at his compliment, though in this light he probably can't see it. 'It's called a Bardot top, after the actress, Brigitte? They started coming out a few years ago and I love the way that they're flattering on almost everyone. Zara are still doing them so I picked this up last week.' Rafael nods politely. 'You don't care where I bought my top.'

'You never know. I might want to get one myself.'

He looks fine in his own clothes. Now that we've spent so much time together, I can see that he's got a sort of uniform: jeans or shorts with a button-down shirt, usually with some sort of pattern (tiny flowers or ice cream cones or alligators). He always looks like he's ready to meet your mum or go to the beach. Maybe meet your mum at the beach.

We've got the whole restaurant nearly to ourselves. There's one other couple at a corner table, but they've got their coffees already.

The waitress comes over but instead of giving us menus, she recites the options. 'Your starters are chicken goujons, Thai egg rolls or arancini balls.'

'Arancini . . .?' I ask.

'Fried rice balls,' she says. 'Then, for the main course, there's fish and chips, lasagne and chips or roast chicken and chips. Do you know what you'd like?'

A cholesterol tablet?

'Is there a wine list?' Rafael asks.

'There's house red or house white. Or champagne. House champagne.'

'I am so sorry about this,' I say when we've sent her off with our choices. 'They made it sound like this was going to be fine dining.'

Rafael smiles. 'At least there are no mushrooms on the menu. That would be suspicious.'

'Or turkey twizzlers.'

'Are you noticing a theme?' he asks.

'A deep fat fryer? And I was really looking forward to a good meal.' My tummy rumbles in agreement.

'*Mi corazón*, it doesn't matter. We're here, let's make the most of it.'

That's music to my ears. Unfortunately, the sounds coming from my tummy aren't nearly as soothing. Neither are the cramps that start pinching my gut. Before the wine even arrives, I know I need the loo. Promptly.

'Will you excuse me? I just need to pop upstairs for a minute. Be right back.'

How embarrassing.

Another cramp nearly doubles me over as I'm going up the stairs towards our room. Perspiration is popping out all over.

At least I make it to the loo.

This is bad. This is really bad. I'm hoping against hope that it's a one-off. Nerves, maybe. That *can* happen.

I just knew there was something in that pool water. I must have swallowed some vile little organism. I should have listened to my instincts, even if getting to lie there in the water, with Rafael holding me, was exactly what I've been hoping for.

Now I'm paying for it.

He'll definitely be wondering where I am by now. It's

reasonable for a date to 'pop upstairs' to change her contacts, for example, or have a quick wee or take an antibiotic that she's only just remembered, or even file a broken nail if it's really bothering her. I'm way beyond hangnail territory now. Unless I've come up here for a nap, I can only be doing one thing.

The starters have probably come. Frying a few chicken strips won't take the kitchen very long. But I'm not exactly in a position to go back downstairs.

Every time I dare start hoping that I've seen the back of the worst of it, another bout hits me like a sledgehammer.

Then, just when I think I'll have to spend the night on the loo and it can't get any worse, it does, because two things happen at once. My courtesy flush, well, doesn't flush, and I hear someone coming into our room.

'It's just me,' Rafael calls through the (thankfully closed) door. 'Are you okay?'

I flush again. The toilet only makes a pathetic little wheeze.

This can't be happening.

'I'm, erm, a little indisposed at the moment.' Understatement of the year. 'Can you please go back downstairs?'

'Oh, right, of course, sorry!' he says. 'Do you need anything?'

A plunger. 'No, I'm fine. See you soon.'

But, clearly, I'm not fine because, an hour later, I've only just left the loo to curl up on the bed. Then I hear the key in the lock again. 'Hello?' Rafael calls, slowly opening the bedroom door. 'Are you okay?'

I am the definition of not okay. 'I'm afraid I'm ill.'

He sits carefully on the bed. Luckily, since the mattress is made of concrete, it doesn't jiggle me.

'I'm so sorry,' I say. 'This is such crap timing.' I can't even muster the strength to admire my own bad pun. 'This doesn't feel like it's going to get better any time soon. I'm sorry,' I say again. Because I really, truly, am so sorry that this is happening. 'Given the, erm, circumstances, I think you might want to get another room. I'll pay for it, of course.'

'Don't be silly,' he says. 'You shouldn't worry about that.'

The very idea of him in here with me when I . . . Ugh. 'No, I'm afraid you *really* need to get your own room.'

'I mean that I'll pay for the room,' he says, 'though I don't really want to leave you in case you need anything. I'll see if there's a room next door.'

'Definitely don't stay next door. That would almost defeat the purpose. I don't want you . . . in the vicinity, if you see what I mean. God, this is so embarrassing.'

He takes my clammy hand in his warm one. 'Don't be embarrassed. It happens to everyone at some point.'

Maybe, but probably not on their very first sleepover with the person they love.

Oh, God, I really do love him, don't I? This is actually happening.

Once again, Nelly, impeccable timing.

'It's better if you're down the hall,' I tell him. 'Or on

another floor. Believe me.' Weighing up where I am in the loo rota, I think I've got a few minutes before the next shift.

'Can I get you anything to help? Some Coke, maybe, to settle your tummy? Or some bread or something? Chips?'

'Urgh, the thought of anything makes me . . . No, thanks. I think I'm better off emptying out rather than filling up. Ooh, speaking of which . . .'

'Right, sorry. I'll go see about another room.'

Gently, so gently, he kisses my sweaty forehead.

By the time I climb into the four-poster bed later, crampy and sick, I'm feeling dreadfully sorry for myself. I'm never ordering Thai takeaway again. In a single portion of leftover rice, I've gone from romance to poomance.

I only hope Rafael can't hear me through the wall.

Later, he texts me.

It makes me feel sick knowing that you are not well, mi corazón. I would do anything to make you better. If I could take this from you, I would. In a way, maybe I am, because I feel everything that you feel.

Well, that's a nice sentiment, but, somehow, I doubt that.

Until I can hold you again,x know that every moment that you walk into a room brings a smile to me. Every time you speak, I feel so much love. I rejoice every day that you spend in my life. Everything you do, everything that you are, is a gift to all who've ever met you. I am so grateful that you've given this gift to me.

PS There's more loo roll outside your door

Chapter 15

Well, if there's any silver lining from the weekend, it's that now I'll have no trouble fitting into my wedding dress. The bad news is that I'm sure I was so vile that Rafael may be having second thoughts about even fake-marrying me.

In fairness, I didn't think I'd be toxic by the morning we left the hotel. The same couldn't be said of my en suite (I did leave the maid a big tip). There'd been so much . . . let's call it evacuation. I mean like mandatory, apocalyptic, 100%, not-a-soul-left-behind evacuation. I really thought I'd be fine on our drive back.

How wrong could I be? Halfway home, the cramps started up again. Singing along to Shakira didn't help. If anything, every wriggle loosened more painful waves.

'I'm sorry,' I'd finally had to tell Rafael. 'Can you please pull over?'

Rafael couldn't have manoeuvred faster if he'd been a Grand Prix driver heading for the pit with the back of his car in flames. Either way, I'm sure he feared the car would need hosing down.

I hurried into the too-low weeds beside the road while Rafael did his best to shield me from the passing lorries. Several honked their amusement as I mortified myself.

I could barely look at him the rest of the way home. I'm horrified now just knowing he's in the same office building. Of course, I've told absolutely no one the true story. Anyone on Instagram would think we spent the entire weekend in loved-up bliss, not in separate rooms with Rafael leaving more loo rolls outside my door every few hours.

And now Jenny won't stop talking about a hen do. 'Really, you don't have to,' I tell her again. Something doesn't sit right about making my friends spend money under false pretences. Ironic, right, considering the whole situation?

I suppose this way, though, everyone would get to meet Rafael before the wedding. I did ring my friends to tell them about my sudden groom-swap (the Approved Version of events), and even managed to deflect most of their questions with declarations of happiness at the sudden turn of events.

Hopefully, wherever we go for the hen do will be loud enough to drown out any more probing questions.

'But I'd really like to do it for you,' Jenny says as I follow her into the office kitchen. 'Cup of tea?'

'Thanks, the peppermint, please.'

She pops the kettle on. 'Everyone would love to celebrate

with you and since you said yourself that Mabs isn't planning anything . . .' She makes a face to be sure I know how she feels about that. 'I can do it, so you may as well stop arguing. Rafael shouldn't be the only one who gets a last blowout.'

'Fine, if you're sure you want to. But please make it something low-key and not expensive.'

'Got it, no private helicopters to Ibiza with male prozzies, then. Where are you going for your honeymoon? I never even asked.'

I freeze. Engaged people would definitely have discussed that by now. Assuming they were really engaged. 'You know Rafael, he always books at the last minute,' I tell her, really hoping that's true. 'We'll do something spontaneously. Maybe camping.'

Jenny splutters her tea. 'You?'

I shrug. 'The things we do for love.'

'Uh-huh.' She's frowning as she stares out the window. 'Erm, Nelly? You probably don't want to see this, but you should.'

I hesitate to join her. Nothing good ever started with the words, 'You probably don't want to see this.'

I look down at the pavement in front of our office building. 'What the hell is he thinking?!'

It takes me seconds to fly down the stairs, with Jenny trailing behind.

'What do you think you're doing?' I hiss at Matt. He's standing in front of a huge bed sheet. 'This is where I work!' No matter how hard I yank at the sheet (which, incidentally, I recognise from his bed), he's got it tied too tightly to the slender trees. I'd need scissors to cut it. Or a saw for those trees. At this point it's either them or me.

Matt looks very proud of his efforts. I reread the words painted in bright blue across the sheet, in case it doesn't say what I think it does.

I LOVE YOU, NELLY.
WILL YOU STILL MARRY ME?

There's no misunderstanding that.

When I see Martha, she gives me a cheery wave. Photo Matt's thumbs-up just adds insult to injury. This is getting better and better. 'What are you two doing here?'

'Matt rang me,' Martha says. 'Don't mind us! Act natural. And don't look at the camera.'

'Matt, really,' I say in what I hope sounds like a not-at-all-hysterical tone. 'You don't need to do this.'

He fiddles with something in the pocket of his sweat-shirt. 'Obviously I do, Nelly, to show you how serious I am.' Suddenly, Bryan Adams starts playing from his pocket.

I recognise the opening piano notes of '(Everything I Do) I Do It For You'. The man has brought his own soundtrack.

'Matt, don't. Please, you're embarrassing yourself.' Not to mention me.

He holds up his hand, but instead of saying anything,

he seems to be punctuating Bryan Adams's words with meaningful looks. He's nodding his head to the music.

Finally, after nodding through about half the song, he says, 'It's like this was written for us.'

I swear, when I look over at Martha, she's singing along. This cannot be happening.

'Where's your boyfriend?' he asks. He scans the windows above us. When I do the same, I see most of my colleagues staring down at me.

'You shouldn't want people to see this, Matt. You're embarrassing yourself.'

'I don't care. Where's Romeo?'

'Should I ring him?' Jenny asks me. 'What? Just trying to be helpful.'

The last thing I want is for Rafael to have to be part of this.

But it's too late, because before I know it, he's beside me. Martha must be eating this up. 'Hi, Matt,' he says. I've got no idea how he can sound so chilled.

'What's up?' Matt answers.

'You know, just working. What's up with you?' Rafael glances at the sign. 'Nice artwork.'

Photo Matt's assistant is catching every word with her fuzzy microphone.

'Thanks. It's from the heart.'

There's a pause between songs. Then Aerosmith comes on, and I hate to break it to Steven Tyler, but I do, very much, want to miss this thing.

'All our favourite songs for the wedding,' Matt says to me. 'We picked them out together,' he explains to the little crowd that's starting to gather around us.

Actually, I didn't particularly like this song. Or most of the Bryan Adams that he put on the soundtrack.

'Matt. I'm getting married in a month. To Rafael.'

'You won't go through with it. He might be all . . .' He points at Rafael. 'Tall and stuff, but you love me. You'll realise that. I know you will.'

'I'm going back to work now, so you might want to pack up your display. Martha, can I have a quick word?'

Rafael and I walk around the corner with Martha. 'I'm not sure that this is the kind of thing we want in the feature,' I tell her.

'But it has to be,' she says. 'Don't you see how perfect it is? Nelly, this is going to be the most romantic piece we've ever done. Readers won't be able to get enough. People would kill for this kind of hook. It's the best publicity we could have hoped for.'

I really thought it was when I started all this.

Rafael takes my hand. 'If it's me you're worried about, don't be. Listen to Martha. This is what you wanted, *mi corazón*, isn't it?'

'I guess so.'

Chapter 16

Oxford Street is heaving with shoppers as Martha and I hurry towards the department store to meet Mabs. I'm not rushing because I want to meet her. And I definitely don't want to go bridesmaid's dress shopping with her. The sooner we start, the sooner we'll be finished.

My phone rings again. Sighing, I send Matt's call to voicemail. Isn't that just the way? When I think back to all the times that I'd have loved for him to ring me. Not just when I practically wore out Rowan's sofa flipping and flopping, tossing and turning while I waited for him to come to his senses on that beach in Spain.

It's fair to say that Matt wasn't always the most communicative of boyfriends. Whereas I'd ring him just to see how he was doing or what he had for lunch or if he got to work on time despite thinking he was going to be late, his calls were more practical. And, it's fair to say, less frequent

What does he think he's playing at now, a month before I marry Rafael, using up his call allowance on me?

Now I suspect that our relationship was a bit like

Christmas for me. I loved the idea of it. I anticipated the closeness and the fun and the steady comfort of knowing I'd found The One. But the reality didn't always measure up. What should have been easy was sometimes fraught. The bond that I so valued sometimes felt weaker than I'd have liked. The good times didn't always outweigh the bad and, if I'm honest, there were quite a few things I would have changed if I could have.

Just like Christmas. Every year, come December, I let myself get excited again. Going home for the holidays should be an annual highlight. Instead, it's days of enforced cohabitation while everyone bickers, in our family's version of the grumbler's greatest hits. My brother invariably turns up for forty-eight hours, swanning around and expecting Charles Dickens to serve his lunch. Both my homecoming and my escape mean an uncomfortable journey on an overpacked train, perched in the aisle on my luggage, trying not to break what's inside.

I guess that, with all the wedding planning activity, I didn't realise that I was perched uncomfortably on my relationship too, trying not to break what was inside.

Even with the mobs of people streaming past us, I can feel Martha's eyes watching me. Not only did I think I wouldn't mind this attention when I won the feature contest, I distinctly remember thinking it would be fun to be followed around like a Kardashian.

'What is it?' I snap at Martha, who's watching me.

'Matt again?' She can hardly contain herself.

'Come on or we'll be late.'

The question hangs between us as I stalk towards the shop.

Mabs is already in front. I figured she'd be late because she's on Latin time (Rafael's warning).

She fluffs her hair when she sees us. It falls in shimmery waves down her back. Then she pushes her sunglasses into it. 'Matt's not coming?'

'Matt isn't welcome!' I say.

'I'm sorry, I meant the photographer. But it's interesting that you thought of your ex.' She raises an eyebrow at Martha.

'Let's just get this done,' I tell them. I dislike shopping at the best of times. It's just peachy having to do it with a supermodel who I suspect wants to be the one walking down the aisle with Rafael instead of me.

Mabs gets off the escalator on the second floor. 'Where are you going?' I call to her as Martha and I keep ascending.

'Designer?' she says. 'Where are you going?'

'Seriously.' It seems to take an age to get back to her. That's probably because the impact that this little excursion will have on my already dwindling bank account unfolds in super slo-mo in my imagination. Starting with a letter from my bank and ending with me bringing homemade sandwiches to work for about the next five years.

'I was thinking about something more . . .' What's the word I'm looking for? Oh, yes. Cheap. 'Something more basic.'

'There's nothing basic about me, *chica*.' Then she laughs. 'Don't be so rigid. We will look.'

As I follow her shiny, swinging hair into the designer section, I wonder if I get to pick how she wears it for the wedding. Maybe in a scraped-back librarian bun. Serve her right.

Mabs darts from rail to rail, exclaiming in Spanish and snatching dresses as she goes. I'm trailing her like a private detective, trying to glimpse the prices without being too obvious. Every time I do, my bank manager probably gets a shiver.

'I'll try these,' she says, handing her bounty to the waiting attendant.

There is a definite theme in her choices. Frantically, I scan the rails. 'I think this one is pretty.' Not that I can afford it, but if I'm to pay a fortune then I want as much material as possible to minimise my cost per square inch.

Mabs is taking a much more minimalist approach. 'Rafael loves short dresses,' she says.

That stops me in my tracks. 'You're not dressing for Rafael.'

Her look tells me the truth. Clearly, she is.

'I want to go upstairs to the proper bridesmaid's dresses,' I tell Martha while Mabs tries on the bandanas masquerading as eveningwear. 'These are ridiculous. It's not what we want for our wedding.'

'Then you should tell her that. Look, I'm not just saying it because conflict makes for a good story. It's your wedding. You should get to make the decisions.'

'I don't suppose you want to tell her?'

Martha laughs. 'I will if you want.'

But we both know I can't let her do that. Mabs is my problem.

'That's so inappropriate,' I tell her when she emerges from the fitting room. Even she's pulling the hem down to try to cover another quarter inch of thigh.

'Why are you being such a . . . such a . . . *Te estás comportando como una monja!*'

'What's that supposed to mean?' Although I can guess from the way she says it. *Monja*. I file that away for later.

She ignores me as she stalks back into the fitting room.

'You may as well not bother trying on the others,' I call after her. 'Because you're not going to wear any of them.'

We ride the escalator in silence to the regular dresses.

'These are so frumpy,' she says once we're there. For all the disdain on her face, she could be looking at a rubbish heap.

'They're not all that bad,' says Martha. 'Sorry, I mean there are some nice ones here.'

With a monumental sigh, Mabs wanders down another rail. 'Hmm, I suppose this isn't bad.' She holds up an off-white lacy number.

She cannot be serious. First of all, it's still almost a thousand quid. For that kind of money, I expect some unpronounceable designer. Secondly, she will not be wearing white to my wedding and, thirdly, I've got shirts that are longer than that dress. 'Why don't you keep looking? I'm thinking more in the two-hundred-pound range. And I'd steer clear of white or off-white too.'

But even I'm having trouble finding anything in my price range. 'I suppose we could try a different shop.' Although I really don't want to drag this out any longer than I need to.

'What, like Phase Eight?' Mabs grimaces. 'Why don't you just put me in a bin bag?'

I'd love to. And how dare she insult Phase Eight! They've got some beautiful dresses.

It's obvious after we've wandered all around the floor a second time that we're never going to agree. That means I'm perfectly justified in making my executive decision. 'This is the one,' I tell Mabs, smiling sweetly. 'Size four, I think?'

Knee-length, high neck, crepe silk layers. She's lucky I don't put her in a cotton housecoat. If she complains, then I'm buying one that goes to the floor. With a cardigan on top. I won't be proud of myself but, so help me, I'll do it.

I've got to put Mabs out of my mind, because tonight is just for Rafael and me. I've got it all planned and it's going to be perfect. I *can* put poomaggedon behind us.

Soho is busy with the after-work crowd. We're all enjoying this week's run of warm weather. I haven't even got a brolly with me, because that's the kind of living-on-the-edge girl I am these days.

My phone rings again as I scan up and down the

narrow street for Rafael. If I don't answer, Matt will only keep trying.

'Yes,' I snap, 'how can I help you?'

'Glad you answered. I was starting to think you were avoiding me.'

'I am avoiding you.'

'Yet you picked up, so clearly you're not. What are you doing?'

'Waiting for Rafael, as it happens. What do you want, Matt?'

'So you're talking to me while you wait for Romeo. Nelly, can't you see what that means?'

I watch the streams of people zigzagging all over the street. 'Only that I've got a few minutes to kill before my fiancé gets here, so if there's nothing else . . .'

Rafael and I catch sight of each other at the same time. His smile is warm enough to keep me cosy during a blizzard. So unlike that best friend of his. But I shove thoughts of Mabs out of my head. The less everyone thinks about her, the better.

'Rafael is here,' I tell Matt. 'I've got to go.'

'See you soon,' he says. I hang up.

Rafael scoops me up into his arms. I'm getting quite used to these greetings now. 'Matt again?' he asks. There's not a jot of worry in his voice. Of course there's not. What on earth could Rafael have to fear from a little competition. He'd win hands down.

Then I remember that Rafael isn't competing for

anything. Why should he be worried when he thinks this is all fake.

That's a downer. 'He wasn't nearly this committed when we were together.'

'He's realising what he's lost,' Rafael says. 'I don't blame him.'

I'm not letting my love-addled brain fall for lines like that, when I know (I know!) it's just part of the charade. 'He's not giving up,' I say. 'I think Martha is encouraging him. She thinks it makes for a better story.' Then I wish I hadn't mentioned that. Because it's no longer just a story. Not for me.

As Rafael holds open the pub door for me, this feels as nerve-wracking as any date I've ever been on.

I get us a bottle of red and we plonk ourselves in the only available chairs, jammed next to each other at the end of a boisterous table. I've got to lean in to talk to him. 'Did Mabs tell you about the dress already?'

He tips his wine glass to mine. 'She said you've been shopping.' He's being very diplomatic. I can just imagine what she told him.

'Does she hate it? The dress?'

'Let's say it's not quite the style she had in mind.' He's sitting so close that I can smell his cologne. Of course it makes me want to bury my face in his neck and sniff. 'But it doesn't matter,' he goes on, unaware of my neck-sniffing urges, 'because the bridesmaid wears what the bride wants, no? She only has to wear it once. She'll get over it.'

'It's not *that* bad, you know. Just for the record, whatever she's told you, I'm not putting her in a postal sack.' Though I'm starting to feel bad about the ruffles. 'And you're right, it's only one day. By the way, what's a *monja*?'

'It's a nun. Why?'

'Oh, no reason.' I just knew Mabs wasn't complimenting me at the dress shop!

As Rafael's hand twiddles the stem of his wine glass, the tendon that runs down from his index finger flexes under his tanned skin. I can't stop imagining kissing it. I really need to have a word with my imagination. 'Have you found your dress?' he asks.

I nod. 'But you're not allowed to know anything about it. It's bad luck.'

I hope the lighting in here is dim enough that he doesn't see me blushing. It's not like he's a proper groom who needs to worry about luck.

'There can't be any bad luck for us,' he says.

Right, because this is all fake. I've got to stop talking like we're really a couple. Much as I want us to be.

'Meeting you has been nothing but good luck,' he says. 'I'm so grateful. Do you know that I nearly didn't meet you that night? I had other plans, well, I double-booked. I cancelled to meet Jenny.'

I take a second to let that sink in. 'Then none of this would have happened.' Despite the noise all around us, I'm nearly whispering. 'We'd never have met.'

'That would have been . . . tragic.' He's staring into my eyes.

'Tragic.' We're inches from each other.

Then his phone starts ringing. Not quietly, either. He's got it on full blast.

He sits straighter to take the mobile from his pocket. The moment skitters away.

'It's just Mabs,' he says, sending her call to voicemail. But there's no time to hope we'll get the magic moment back, because he starts looking at something on his screen. 'Can you excuse me for a minute?'

'Sure.' I need the loo anyway, though I don't ever plan to use that word in front of Rafael again.

I'm about to get up when he says, 'I'll be— Just . . .' Without another word he goes outside.

What's he doing out there? Is he ringing Mabs back? No, he's looking at his phone. Pacing. Scrolling through something. Something for work, maybe. His clients can get in touch any time. It looks like bad news. One of them must be pissed off.

He's back at the table when I return from the loo. 'Is everything okay?'

'Yes, fine.' He tops up our wine glasses. 'I'm hungry. Should we get something quickly to eat? Then I should head off.'

'Oh, sure, yes, okay.' So much for tonight being a date. He's probably got a real date after this, with someone he actually wants to kiss.

How can I, in my right mind, let myself feel what I do for him? It's delusional. At least with Matt I've only recently realised that our relationship wasn't quite as solid as I'd hoped. With Rafael, I know this is all for show. If it weren't for my British passport, he would have no reason even to be speaking to me.

I may as well face it. No matter how I feel about Rafael, this is just a business transaction for him.

How many ways does he have to show me that before it sinks in?

Chapter 17

Just try acting all loved-up when your heart is turning inside out. But that's the thing about this feature. It's not concerned with what's actually happening. We're feeding the illusion, making our lives better than real. We're the most romantic couple in the country. Isn't everyone just blissful?

#noyourecrying.

If I don't get a grip and put my feelings aside, then all this will be for nothing. Rafael will run a mile (back to Colombia, as he'll have no permission to stay), there'll be no wedding and I'll end up living with cats and retiring from my office job after forty years of mediocre service. People will remember me as that woman who kept to herself and once had ambitions. One or two may recall something about an ex-boyfriend and a bed sheet.

I can't let that happen. I'll just have to deal with the heartbreak later. That's bound to make me a barrel of laughs on the honeymoon.

'Have you heard anything back from the Home Office

yet?' I ask Rafael as we make our way to meet Martha. She wants to see us picking out all the decorations for the reception. Even though I've known for months what I want.

See what I mean? None of this is real.

He sighs as he shakes his head.

'That must be good, then.' When I updated the registry office about the groom-swap, they said they'd have to let the Home Office know, since Rafael isn't a citizen yet. We haven't got to wait for approval or anything to go ahead with the wedding, but they might have had questions. I guess this means they don't. 'You're not worried, are you?'

He grasps my hand. 'Of course not. It's just the normal bureaucracy. It will be fine.'

I should be over the moon to step into Wedding Wonderland (and Party Central). The enormous warehouse is stuffed full of every wedding decorator's dream: aisle upon aisle of frilly, frothy, chic, sleek and playful décor, vases, candelabras, silk flowers, birdcages, lanterns, bunting, confetti, feathers, fairy lights and everything else one can imagine.

Yet the happy little bubble I manage to build around Rafael's words deflates as soon as we get inside.

My balloon pops because Mabs is standing beside Martha. She's fiddling on her phone. Probably Instagramming more snide quote marks about me.

'Cariño!' She drapes herself over Rafael to kiss his cheeks. I can't help but notice his arm sliding around her waist.

She makes a half-hearted gesture towards me. 'Hello, Nelly.' I know a passive-aggressive air-kiss when I see one.

When Martha and I air-kiss too, I worry that this is going to become a thing we have to do now each time we meet.

'Are you ready?' Martha asks. 'It would be nice to get some footage of you strolling up and down the aisles, maybe fooling around with some of the props. Like those, maybe?' She points to the wall display of silly hats and masks. 'Were you thinking of a photo booth?'

'No,' I say.

'That's a great idea!' says Rafael.

'Love it,' Mabs adds, like she's got any say at all.

'I don't know, it seems a bit silly.'

'What's wrong with being silly at our wedding, *mi corazón?* Aren't we supposed to have fun?'

'That's not the point,' I say. Everyone waits for me to tell them what *is* the point of a wedding, then. 'I just mean that I've got an idea about how it should look.' Glancing at the long table beside us, I say, 'Look at these. Big, romantic flowers like these on the tables and gorgeous vintage linen, loads of candles, that sort of thing. Romantic.'

Rafael takes one of the props off the wall and holds it to his face. 'No moustaches?'

'Muy romántico.' Mabs laughs.

He adds a pair of thick black-framed glasses, then crosses his eyes. 'I bet you can't wait to walk down the aisle with me now.'

Martha is beaming. She's loving this.

'Come on, be serious,' I say. Rafael bounces his moustache

up and down. 'Have you got any, I don't know, visions in your head about what the wedding would look like?'

He thinks for a second. 'Definitely something colourful. Like Carnival.'

All I remember from Carnival in Notting Hill is half-naked dancers and not being able to find a loo. 'You mean like sequins? Feathers?'

'That's perfect!' says Mabs, though Rafael could have suggested a come-as-your-favourite-infection theme and she'd have backed him up.

'I've got an idea,' Martha says, 'if you don't mind me butting in. This might be easier if you can actually visualise what each of you is thinking, so why don't you both go around separately and pick everything you like? Then you can put it all together and show each other.' She looks very pleased with herself as she wheels two empty shopping trolleys back to where we're standing.

Mabs links her arm through Rafael's. 'I'll help you, *cariño*. I know exactly what you like.'

Before we go our separate ways, though, Rafael sidles up to me. Unfortunately, Mabs is still hanging on him, and where he goes, she goes. He plants a gentle kiss on my lips. 'See you in a few minutes.'

I smile at Mabs just before she turns away. She pretends she doesn't see my smugness, but I know she does.

The clicks from Photo Matt's camera follow me down the aisles. I'm in shabby chic heaven. There's enough bunting here to kit out every teashop in the country. My cart is nearly full before I even get to the floral section. I've picked out mercury glass candleholders and pressed glass bottles, wooden picture frames that I have no idea what I'd do with, gorgeous lace tablecloths, olden-days suitcases (ditto on the no idea), wooden flower crates, hand-lettered signs and, of course, birdcages. Then I pile the cart with enough silk flowers to festoon one of Rafael's Carnival floats. In tasteful colours, though.

There's no sign of him when I get back to Martha. 'That was quick,' she says.

'I've got a theme in mind.' We both look at the lovely pale pinks, creams and silvers in my cart.

'Very nice,' she says. 'I just saw Rafael go down the flower aisle. Before they come back, how do you feel about doing a reveal of your themes with each other? If you set up your things over there, I can put Rafael around that corner so you can't see what each other has picked.'

'You mean like that *Don't Tell The Bride* programme? Sure, I'm game.' Better to give Rafael the full effect anyway. It's kind of hard to see how beautiful everything is when it's jumbled together in the cart.

I'm snapping a few Instagrammable photos when I hear Mabs and Rafael coming back. Even if I understood more than three words of Spanish, I'd have no chance with those two. They're rabbiting on a mile a minute.

Instead of doing what Martha asks, though, Rafael comes around the corner about 30 seconds later, pushing his cart. 'This way we see each other's at the same time,' he reasons. Then he skids to a stop and throws his hands over his eyes. 'Are you ready?'

'I'm ready. Let's see what you've got.'

He stares at my display while I gawp at his cart.

It looks like a bag of Skittles has detonated in there. He's thrown armloads of tablecloths in, all with clashing patterns: blue stripes, purple checks, pink flowers and, for some reason, monkeys and alligators.

I don't see so much as one tasteful rose amidst the riot of bright tropical silk flowers. There are packs of coloured balloons and streamers, huge pink, orange, green and blue tissue paper flowers, masks with feathers . . . and a selection of moustaches.

He's pointing underneath the cart at the candy floss machine. 'Everyone will love this. And the donut wall, though we'll have to order that separately, I guess? And I was thinking drums. We could have a bongo bar. People could jam. What do you think?'

I think it would be perfect, if we were throwing a full-moon party.

I know what's happened. This is another translation error. He's mistaking our wedding for a six-year-old's birthday party.

He and Mabs are examining my very tasteful display. 'What do you think?' Martha asks them both.

Mabs does a huge yawn. Whether it's real or not, her point is unmistakable. 'Sorry, I was out late last night,' she claims.

'It's a different look than I was thinking of,' Rafael says more diplomatically.

That was exactly the word I was going to use about the affront to the eyes that he's put together.

'I'm guessing that matches your dress?' he adds.

I get an awful thought. 'Does that match what you're going to wear?'

He nods happily. I haven't the heart to ask whether he'll be turning up in pink, orange, green or blue. Or maybe purple checks.

This is hopeless. Not only am I going to be the most heartbroken bride ever to walk down the aisle, our wedding will look like it's been catered by Ronald McDonald.

'Look how far apart we are!' I tell him. 'We've only got three weeks. We're never going to put something together that doesn't look like a dog's dinner.'

He's at my side in an instant. '*Mi corazón, estoy enamorado de ti*. That's all that matters. We'll figure out the rest together.'

Martha gushes. She obviously speaks more Spanish than I do.

'What did you say?'

'I said I'm in love with you,' Rafael tells me.

Mabs's expression is perfectly blank.

'Very good,' I whisper into his ear

'It's authentic,' he whispers back.

But it's not, I remind myself again when he grabs my hand. It's not authentic at all.

Chapter 18

If anyone had asked me to imagine the perfect hen party, my description would have included champagne and string quartets, whispering waitstaff, vintage teapots and enough clotted cream to slather the entire county of Devon two times over.

But nobody asked me, because hen parties aren't about the bride. They're about the person organising it. In this case, to my horror, that's turned out to be Mabs. I distinctly remember telling Jenny that Mabs wasn't involved, so I'm still unclear about how she went from selfish and disinterested to life-of-the-party planner.

Jenny has fallen under her spell, but her fake perfection doesn't fool me. Just because she's remembering everyone's names and making sure nobody goes without a drink or someone to talk to. I know what she's really like. She wouldn't have brought everyone to a Latin music club if she wasn't trying to show me up.

'Ah, merengue,' she cries when a new song comes on. 'Come, it's easy, I'll teach you.' With a huge smile, she starts pulling everyone onto the dance floor. 'Nelly?' She holds her hand out to me.

I'm wracking my brain for an excuse – an old trick knee or surprise case of vertigo? – when, suddenly, I'm spun completely around. 'Let me teach you, *mi corazón.*' Rafael is smiling down at me in his arms.

I will give Mabs a speck of credit for combining my party with Rafael's. Though I suspect she wasn't thinking of me when she did that.

I hate to admit it, but the music is catchy. At least I can hear the beat to this one.

'All you do is move your hips, like this, when you step.' I can feel the warmth of his hands on my hips as he gently guides them. 'Like this. That's it.' Everyone else is dancing in lines, but Rafael is facing me. Our bodies are inches apart. 'That's it, nice and easy,' he says. 'Good.'

Wow, this is sexy. If I'd known that Latin dancing was nothing but standing-up foreplay, you could have signed me up long ago.

Jenny cries 'Woo hoo, go, Nelly!' when she spots us. Then she steps backwards, right onto Rowan's foot. 'Sorry!' she cries. Ouch. Rowan's in open-toed shoes too.

Then, too quickly, the song ends. There's a split second when Rafael and I are face to face. He's looking into my eyes with that easy smile playing on his lips. I want to stay in this place forever, where magazine features and ex-fiancés and gorgeous best friends don't exist. Where it's just me and Rafael and this isn't an agreement between us, but something that's real. That's what I want so badly.

Rafael leans in slowly and kisses me.

I'm lost in that kiss.

'Sorry,' he murmurs.

'Don't be,' I say. 'It's our hen do.'

'You mean our stag party.'

'What do they call it when we're both here?'

He shrugs. 'Perfect.'

But Mabs isn't about to let us be perfect together. 'Our song,' she tells Rafael. She's swaying her hips to the rhythm. Even I'm mesmerised watching her. 'Do you still want to dance with me? *Me permite*,' she says to me.

She doesn't wait for my *permite*, though. They sweep onto the floor together in, it seems, a single fluid motion and begin a dance that looks choreographed just for them. Their bodies are in perfect sync with one another as they move with the music. He spins her. She doesn't even seem to be thinking about what she's doing. When they come back together, their hands find each other's hips, backs, arms.

It's so sensual that I can barely watch. I feel my face flame. Everyone must be thinking the same thing. That they've definitely had sex with each other.

She holds on to his hand when the song ends, making a face that probably usually means she gets her way, but not this time. He comes off the dance floor anyway.

Then he holds out his hand to me. 'Our turn.'

'Oh, no, really, I don't know how.'

'I'll show you, *mi corazón*, trust me.'

I'm about as keen as a prisoner on death row as he leads me to the floor.

'Really, I don't know how to do this.'

He won't stop smiling. 'Just follow me. Feel my hands. They tell you what to do.'

Sure enough, when he goes forward, his warm hand in mine pushes gently while the one around my waist pulls back. 'See? Easy.' Slowly, he spins me. I don't even trip over my feet! His hand moves from my back to my hip. 'Move your hips, like this.' He demonstrates while his hand grasps my hip.

But even with this private lesson (which is far from private, but I'm trying not to think about everyone watching us), I feel like a wooden-legged oaf. I am the Zamboni that comes to clean up the ice after the world-class skater has just nailed the world's first quadruple axel.

'Would you have married Mabs if she'd had a passport?' I ask him.

He doesn't break his rhythm, which is more than I can say for myself. I seem to be to-ing when I should be fro-ing. I just want this song to end. 'Where did that come from?' he asks.

'Just . . . answer.'

'Well, yes, it would have been a no-brainer. But she doesn't have a passport and I'm marrying you.'

That doesn't exactly make me feel better.

I don't get the chance to dwell on it, though, which is probably good, because my friends surround us when the song changes. I'm trying not to feel too terrible for cutting them off these past few months. They're here now. That's the kind of friends I'm lucky enough to have: the kind that don't hold grudges and will definitely keep Mabs in line if I need them to.

'Remind me how Mabs got involved with this?' I ask Jenny later, pointing my chin at the other end of the bar where she's standing with Jenny's boyfriend, Rafael and a few of his coaching friends.

'Drink,' she says, nodding to the mojito she's just handed me. 'She rang Ed and suggested we all do something together. Why, do you mind? Would you rather it had been just us girls?'

'No, no, it's more fun with everyone together. I just wondered, that's all.'

'That's *not* all.' She's giving me the same look she gives the insurance salespeople when they try to take shortcuts on the paperwork. 'What's wrong?'

'Nothing. Really.' Now I've gone and made her suspicious. That's the last thing we need. 'Can I tell you a secret? I don't really like Mabs.'

'Psh, no kidding!' she says, swigging her drink. 'What's there to like about a glamazon who's practically glued to the side of your fiancé? I think you're being remarkably tolerant about it.'

'Cheers,' I say. That makes me feel better.

Chapter 19

The whole plan starts unravelling on a Monday. Such a state of affairs really does just confirm it as my least favourite day of the week.

I'm right in the middle of one of the most complicated pension-enrolment forms when Jenny turns up at my desk with a funny look on her face. 'Lunch in an hour?' I say, barely looking up. 'I've got one more of these bastards to finish first.'

'Someone's here to see you,' she says.

That explains the funny look. Rafael must have wrapped up his client meeting early. 'Why didn't he just come in?' Though he hasn't ventured into my office since the day he outed us in front of all my colleagues.

'Mabs is here too,' she says.

We're not supposed to have non-staff on the floor because of all the confidential information. It still doesn't explain why Mabs would be with Rafael during the workday. Now my expression matches Jenny's as I go to find out what's going on.

Mabs isn't with Rafael, though. She's with Matt. The office door clicks shut behind me. Whatever this is about, the less my colleagues hear, the better. 'What do you need, Matt?' I think I've been admirably restrained whenever he's around, given that I want to shout at him to leave me alone.

'I need to talk some sense into you,' Matt says, 'before it's too late.'

'And you're here because . . .?' I say to Mabs. 'Shouldn't you be at work?' I need to get them out of here before he blows my cover in front of Mabs.

'It's more important when a friend needs help.' She says this with a perfectly straight face. Like she's his emotional support weasel.

'Rafael and I are just fine, thank you, so I'm sorry you've wasted the trip. Matt, really, you have to stop this. You're the one—' I catch myself just in time. My eyes slide to Mabs. 'You're the one who needs to see sense.'

Matt shakes his shaggy head. He still hasn't shaved or cut his hair since coming back from Spain. I wonder if it's some kind of scruffy protest. 'You were hurt when I went to Spain, Nelly. I get that and I know it wasn't the most mature response, but I really just needed time to think. I didn't leave you. I never left you. I'm sorry.'

Despite everything, I find myself softening towards him. I know how I would feel if my fiancé suddenly announced he was marrying someone else. 'Thank you.'

Mabs's eyes dart between us. 'Does that mean you forgive Matt?' she asks me.

'I'm still angry, but, yes, I forgive him. That doesn't mean I'm changing my mind about the wedding, though, so, I'm sorry, but you're wasting your time.'

'Marry me instead!' says Matt.

'You don't even want to get married,' I remind him. I can see that so clearly now. I could barely get him to commit to staying at my place on the weekend. He always took his toothbrush back home with him. I wish I'd read the toothpaste in the sink long ago. 'If you remember, that's why you ran away to Spain in the first place.'

'I realised my mistake,' he says. 'I want to marry you now.'

'You do not. Matt, really, you don't. You proposed because I'd been hinting about it for a year, not because you wanted to marry me. You just don't want me marrying someone else now, and I'm sorry about that, but Rafael and I are doing this.'

'I should never have broken up with you,' he says, shaking his shaggy head again.

Mabs jumps on that like it's the last half-price Chloé bag in the sale, but I can't think fast enough to head her off. 'Matt broke up with you?' she asks. 'I thought you broke up with him when you told him about Rafael.'

'She did tell me about him after we broke up,' he says. 'That was a shock.'

'I bet it was,' she says, staring at me. 'When did you say you and Rafael got together?'

I will not cave in under her annoyingly lash-perfected

gaze. 'Not till after Matt and I ended things. We met six months ago, though, through work. I went upstairs to sort out an account he'd messed up—'

She waves her hand at me. 'Yes, I know, I read that in the article. I just keep wondering why Rafael never said anything to me all those months. Not a word. He's never done that before.'

'Well, I'm sure he's also told you that nothing happened, so there wasn't anything to tell.'

'Wasn't there?' she asks. 'When you were in love with each other? Rafael has told me about every single one of the women he has fancied.'

That must have irked her. She'd have hated pretending to lend a friendly ear, when it was other parts of her anatomy that wanted to get friendly.

'Did you notice anything?' she asks Matt. 'In all those months, were there any signs that this was happening?'

'Nothing at all,' he says.

At least that's true, considering that Rafael and I didn't really know each other while Matt and I were together. 'But you did know that I'd become friends with Rafael,' I point out to Matt. 'I know I mentioned him.'

He frowns. 'I don't remember that.'

'I definitely did, because we did things together. As friends.' I cannot believe that I've stooped to gaslighting my ex.

Mabs doesn't look convinced, either. 'Doesn't it seem strange that the woman who you're closest to in the whole world could have fallen for another man and not drop any clues at all? Especially if, as Nelly claims, she was *doing things* with Rafael?'

Who could miss that double entendre? It's time to end this interrogation. 'I'd love to rehash the end of our relationship with you, but I'm afraid I've got work to do, so if there's nothing else?'

I'm just about to slide my key card to open the office door when Matt says, 'None of this would be happening if I hadn't called off the wedding.'

'*You* called it off?' Mabs asks. She stares at me.

My laugh sounds fake even to me. It's not helping that Ms Marple there thinks she's solved the mystery. 'Well, come on, Matt, you said yourself that you just got cold feet. It wasn't an end, you said. You had to go off and think, remember? Then I ended it when I told you about Rafael.'

'How very convenient that that's when you and Rafael decided you were in love and getting married,' Mabs says. 'After being so innocent all that time. Except I don't think that's what happened. Is it, Nelly?'

I'm not saying anything that could harm my defence later.

'I think that you and Rafael both need this wedding,' she goes on, 'and that's why you're marrying each other. Am I right?'

'You're imagining things, Mabs,' I say. 'We're in love. I'm sorry if that's uncomfortable for either of you, but it's the truth. Now, some of us have to work.'

My hand is shaking so much that I can barely get my key card through the swipe. This is bad. This is very bad.

Back on my floor, I ring Rafael from the loo but it goes straight through to voicemail. 'It's me. Mabs and Matt were just here and I think they're suspicious. Mabs definitely is, so give me a ring when you get this so we can figure out how to . . .' How to what, exactly? Rewind time so that we're not two virtual strangers lying to everyone we know? 'What to say.'

Chapter 20

Playing back Martha's message again doesn't make it sound any less ominous. 'When you get a minute, can you please give me a ring? A few things have come to light and I just I need to clarify . . . so please ring me back when you get this.'

Nothing good *comes to light*. Infidelities and suspicious lumps come to light. Mabs must have said something. Or maybe Matt. It doesn't matter who the Judas was. This is exactly what I've been afraid of.

What on earth made me think we could pull this off? This is big, not like substituting own-brand crisps or light mayonnaise for regular. I'm trying to pass off a whole phony husband to everyone we know. I should have known that Mabs would be looking for anything to stop Rafael marrying someone else. To be fair, I'd do exactly the same thing in her shoes.

The longer I wait to ring Martha back, the more questions she'll have. 'Sorry to bother you after work hours,' I say when she picks up. 'But your message sounded urgent?'

'Thanks for ringing back,' she says. 'It's about the feature. I just wanted to clarify a few things on the background, if that's okay? I've been talking with Matt . . .'

So it wasn't Mabs. 'Sure, happy to answer any questions, but, can I ask why it's relevant now?'

'Oh, well I guess only because we've pitched you and Rafael as a fairy-tale romance and we've already published the piece about how you met, so we want to be sure we've not misled our readership in any way. I'm sure you understand.'

'Of course, of course. Fire away, then.' Hopefully my tone sounds bright and breezy and not at all like my stress level might be trying to give me a heart attack.

'You said that you and Rafael met months before you and Matt broke up.'

'Yep.' That is definitely what I said. So far, no lies.

'But, well, Matt didn't know anything about Rafael, not even that you'd become friends. Presumably you must have spent time together, to have fallen in love, so how did you keep all that from Matt when he was your boyfriend? No, your fiancé?'

'I didn't keep anything from him,' I said. 'Matt's been pretty busy this last year with work. Before he took his sabbatical to go to Spain, I mean. I'm not surprised if he doesn't remember everything about my social life. We often did things separately, with our own friends, I mean.' All true, every word of it.

'This has put me in a difficult position, Nelly,' she says.

'Because Matt actually went over my head to my boss. It's raising some concern about the feature. I want to assure you that I believe you, but . . .'

'But your boss doesn't,' I finish for her. 'I understand. It's my word against Matt's. Except . . . What if I had some pictures from when Rafael and I were together? Before, I mean. Would that help?'

'I thought you didn't?'

That's a very good point. 'Well, no, I don't . . . but I think my sister-in-law might. She was with us sometimes. Because they weren't dates or anything. Do you want me to check?' Oh, boy. Now I'm involving Rowan.

'That would be perfect, Nelly, thanks. I'm sure my boss would be satisfied then.'

'But these aren't for publication, right?'

'No, no, the rest of the series is all about the wedding. Besides, it might not play well to make too much of the fact that you and Rafael met while you were still with Matt. You know how people can be. Even if nothing happened until you were single, some people will still judge.'

It all sounds so plausible that I have to remind myself that it's not true. I never cheated on Matt, never even thought about it, with Rafael or anyone else. I never kept anything from him, either. I didn't even know Rafael existed until after Matt dumped me. I'm only doing this *because* Matt dumped me. It's all pretend.

'I'll try to get Rowan to send me some pics from her phone and I'll send them on to you.'

'Thanks, Nelly, I'm so relieved.'

She's not the only one.

That's why I'm about to throw myself on Rowan's mercy. She's the only one who knows the real story. I've got no other choice.

My nephew, Leo, answers the door. 'What's the password?' He's got a plastic sword in his hand and one of his dad's leather belts looped around his forehead over his sweatshirt hood. The end hangs down between his eyes. It does look a bit like a medieval helmet.

I hold up my bag. 'I brought pudding.'

'That's the password!' he cries. 'What is it?'

'You'll have to wait till after dinner. How about a hug?'

'How about a hint?' But he lets me hug him as his sister launches herself on us both.

I've got a child dragging on each arm as deliciously sharp and tangy aromas draw me into Rowan's kitchen. She's at the open oven. 'I brought wine,' I tell her. 'And two hangers-on.'

'Auntie Nelly brought pudding,' Leo says. 'But she won't tell us what it is.'

I pretend-slap Caitlin's hand away from the bag. 'Patience is a virtue, children. Shall I open this or is there one on the go?'

'Bless you,' she says. 'There's white in the fridge. Open the red if you want. We're having ribs.'

I might only get over here every few months nowadays, but it always feels like home. Rowan and Paul have lived here since before they got married, so in a way I grew up in this house. Especially since it was a home-away-from-home (not to mention laundry-away-from-laundry and fridge-away-from-fridge) while I was at university in London.

'Paul still on assignment?'

Her concentration is absolute as she flips over the sizzling ribs.

'Are you actually still together?' I add. 'I'm not going to find out in a few years that I've got a second sister-in-law, right?'

She closes the oven. 'Still together, for better or worse. He's back next week.'

'He'd better be. I'll kill him if he's not at the wedding.'

Once Caitlin and Leo are sure that the pudding box won't be opened before dinner, they completely lose interest in me. Fickle children.

'You know techy things, right?' I ask Rowan as she sips her wine. 'I mean, that's what you do.'

'Yeah, I'm a techy thing doer.'

'Weren't you promoted to Senior Techy Thing Doer recently? What I mean is that you could, for example, change the date on a photo, maybe backdate it a few months? Is that possible?'

'The question isn't whether it's possible; of course it is. It's why you want to do it.' She waits for my answer.

'Because I think I'm in trouble, Rowan. You know how I sort of fudged the story about how Rafael and I got together?'

'By fudged, you mean completely lied to everyone we know, including a national magazine who could sue you if they find out? Yeah, duck, I know.'

'Right, so when you put it like that, it's even more important that you help me.'

I don't blame her suspicious look. I'd be wary too, if I had a mendacious relative asking for a favour.

'Rafael and I need a few pictures together,' I tell her. 'So that we can show them to the magazine editor . . . and maybe to the Home Office, but I'm guessing about that. If they need evidence about us being together.' Surely that would be better than our original idea: claiming there's no evidence. Though I should probably stop saying evidence if I want Rowan's help.

'Will you come with us to help take them? And then – small thing, really, and I wouldn't ask if I knew how to do it myself – work your magic to backdate them a bit?'

'You want me to forge photographs that the UK government will use as evidence.'

I knew I shouldn't have said evidence so many times. 'Only if they need to!' I say. 'They probably won't. It's really so I've got something to show Martha. My editor. Apparently, Matt has put some doubts in her mind. I could just kill him.'

I can practically see her mind whirring away as she processes this data. 'Which means you're in deep shite,' she says.

'I am!'

'Come here, duck.' She gathers me into her arms. 'I'll help. What are sisters for, if not to go to prison together.'

'At least you wouldn't have to cook every night,' I say.

'That's very tempting.'

Chapter 21

'Are you really sure you want to do this?' I murmur to Rowan as we wait for Rafael in front of Battersea Dogs and Cats Home. 'I know it was my suggestion, but this really is above and beyond.' To be clear, I only asked Rowan to take (and alter) some photos for us.

'Well, you should have thought about that before you opened your big mouth about dogs in front of little ears,' she answers. Leo and Caitlin beam back at me.

Oh, right. I did do that. 'I just thought it would make for nice pictures. I wasn't thinking. I shouldn't have said anything in front of them, I'm sorry. Forgive me?'

'I'll forgive you after you've picked up about a million poos,' she snaps.

'If you get a tiny dog it'll have tiny poos. That won't be so bad.'

My sister-in-law just glares at me.

I watch Rafael as he creeps up behind the children. They both jump when he says, 'Who wants to get a dog today?'

I catch Rowan's face as Rafael kisses me hello. I have

told him that she knows the truth. I guess he's keeping it real in front of the children. Though I really hope that Her Majesty's government wouldn't stoop to making a six-year-old give evidence. Not that it will come to that anyway. And I really must stop saying evidence.

'We probably won't get one today,' Rowan explains in what I've learned is her patient voice. 'We need to go through an assessment first. There's probably lots of paperwork, and then they'll find a dog that they think might be a good fit. Today's just to do the assessment.'

'But we'll be able to play with the dogs, won't we?' Leo asks. He looks a lot less excited by the prospect of paperwork than about being licked in the face.

She smooths his hair. 'I don't know, duck. We'll see.'

Inside isn't at all what I imagined. It looks like a sleek GP's waiting room. Staff in medical uniforms bustle in and out while people fill in forms on clipboards. It even smells vaguely doctorish. There's nothing furry or on four legs in here.

I can tell that the children are disappointed by this too. Hopefully once Rowan fills in the form, they'll let us see some animals. Otherwise I'm definitely going to have to buy ice cream for everyone.

I feel doubly bad when one of the staff members takes Rowan and the kids into another room for an interview. If Caitlin knew the word, her look would definitely say What The F**k.

'Did you have dogs growing up?' I ask Rafael. This is the kind of thing we should know about each other.

'No, only cats. Did you have dogs?'

'And cats,' I tell him. 'But my parents didn't get another one after Picatso died.'

He snorts. 'You did not name a cat Picatso. That is brilliant.'

'Thanks, I am pretty proud of it, actually. I think I was only about ten when we got him. His markings were really asymmetrical, you know, like the paintings. What was your cat's name?'

'Mimi, Cucho, Tigre, Silvestre . . .' He's counting off on his fingers. 'Simba and a bunch of others.'

'Were these all at once or did you just have very bad luck keeping your pets alive?'

'My father can't resist a stray, and the neighbours know it.'

This doesn't surprise me. Rafael is exactly the kind of person who'd be from an animal-rescuing family.

Finally, Rowan comes back out front. 'Ready to meet some dogs?' she asks.

'You passed the test, then?'

She laughs. 'I think the big garden and having Nora there during the day swung it for us.'

Nora is like one of the family at Rowan's. She started as Leo's nanny when Rowan went back to work. She added Caitlin to her rota when she came along, then started doing housework and has never left. I wonder how she's going to feel about adding poo-scooping to her day.

As we open the door to the kennels, the noise washes

over us: excited dogs and excited people. Rowan snatches the back of Leo's shirt just as he grabs Caitlin's hand and starts to run. 'Hold on, let's do this systematically.' Spoken like a true computer programmer. 'Some of the dogs aren't good for kids, remember?'

I don't envy Rowan this job. How are they ever going to pick just one? I want to spring every one of them from their kennels. #cutenessoverload.

Rafael takes his phone out. 'Ready?' We stand in front of one of the kennels while he holds his phone in front of us.

'Wait. Rowan has to take them, remember? We're not supposed to have any.'

'This is for me,' he says. Then he tucks me into his chest with one arm and snaps a photo with his other arm outstretched.

'Hey, that's not bad,' I say, looking at his screen. The springer spaniel behind us is staring straight into the camera with her ears perked up. She's a natural.

'I've got the perfect length,' he murmurs. 'For selfie-taking.'

I'm simultaneously trying not to laugh at the suggestion and imagining who else has snuggled under his arm for photos before.

'Auntie Nelly, why are you wearing a winter coat?' Caitlin asks. 'Aren't you hot?'

I'm wearing a winter coat for the same reason that I've got a bag full of woolly jumpers under my arm and Rafael is sweating in a thick sweatshirt. I've lost about five pounds in water weight since we arrived, but it needs to look like wintertime for the photos. I wipe a trickle of sweat from my forehead. 'It's a photo shoot for Instagram,' I tell her. The whole family knows about my ambitions.

'Rowan, could you take one of us like this again, but with your phone?'

It's not *only* so that I can snuggle back under his arm.

'Got it,' she says, glancing at her phone. 'Keep going. I'll just take a bunch and we'll see what looks good.'

There's a gorgeous husky in one of the kennels. Her ice-blue eyes bore into mine as we're passing.

I lean down with Rafael behind me so that we're both in the shot. 'Hello, pretty girl.'

She comes closer. I feel like we're bonding. 'Come here, my pretty. Aren't you gorgeous?' Her tail starts to wag as she comes up to the bars. Her ears twitch when I start making kissy noises. It's such a great feeling to connect with an animal. 'Hello, pretty.' I read her name from the information board. Hello, Miska, pretty girl. Come here, Miska—'

Her tongue darts out lightning-quick. She drags it straight across my teeth as I'm smiling into the kennel. 'Urghh. Ugghhhhh.' No amount of wiping my teeth erases the feeling of just having been French-kissed by a dog.

'Got it,' Rowan says. 'Action shot.'

'Do it again!' Leo cries. 'That was funny.'

Miska looks pleased with herself.

I keep my face well away from the rest of the dogs as Rowan snaps more photos of Rafael and me together.

There are a few tears when we leave without a new pet, but the children let themselves be cheered by the promise of bowling.

'I can run them a bit towards the Tube, if you'd like,' Rafael offers.

'That would be great,' Rowan says. 'Tire them out. Hold hands!' she shouts after them. All three clamp hands.

'He's really nice,' she says.

'Mmm hmm, he's great.' I can tell she's watching me as we walk along. 'He's actually just about the most perfect man you could imagine.'

'This isn't fake for you,' she says. It's not a question. I could bluff some flippant answer, but Rowan knows me.

'No. But it is for him, so that's that.'

'I'm sorry, duck.'

'It doesn't matter.'

'Smile,' Rowan says as I'm tightening the Velcro on my bowling shoes. They won't let me on the lane without the shoes. I'm glad I've got a bit of a barrier with the woolly socks I'm wearing, even if my feet are dripping. Mmm, that'll be extra-nice for the next person.

Rafael takes out his phone, snapping a photo of Rowan and the kids.

'Too bad we can't use the ones with the children,' I muse as he shows me the photo. 'They're in shorts.' I wish I'd thought to have Rowan bring extra clothes for them.

If I had my way, we'd snap loads of photos holding up

bowling balls and get out of here, but we promised the children they could play . . . right after we snap loads of photos holding up bowling balls.

'We should have drinks, definitely,' I tell Rowan. 'So it looks like night-time.' I order myself a glass of wine and a lager for Rafael.

'You're drinking now?' Leo says to Rafael. 'You're an alcoholic.'

'No, you're an alcoholic.'

'No, you are.'

'No, you are.'

'No, you are.'

'Nobody's an alcoholic,' I say. 'It's after lunchtime. Besides, these aren't for drinking.'

Rafael stops with his pint midway to his lips.

'That's a prop beer,' I tell him. 'Follow me. Rowan, get ready to take a few candids, okay?'

Sauntering between groups of bowling-shoed strangers in the bar area, I find just the kind of people I'm looking for. I duck under Rafael's arm and, turning to the couple beside us, I say, 'Have you been bowling here before? Cheers!' They're too surprised by my sudden interest to be impolite. They raise their glasses to ours. 'Hope you win.'

I count to five in my head before casually leaving the baffled couple. 'I got a nice one of you all clinking glasses,' Rowan tells me.

'Good work,' Rafael says. 'I bet we can get loads of

candids with our friends here.' He gestures around the entire bowling alley. 'Let's try.'

We spend the next half-hour photo-bombing groups of strangers – sitting on their chairs while we pretend to do up our shoes, high-fiving strikes and even buying a round of shots to enjoy with one couple. Those weren't prop shots, either. By the time we leave with Rowan and the children, at least half a dozen of our new friends wave us goodbye.

Chapter 22

We're standing in front of the town hall where, a week from today, we'll marry each other.

It's a beautiful building, with its sandstone façade and wide steps at the front running up to the entrance. Those steps are going to make for a nice photo with everyone after the ceremony.

But we have to get through today first. 'Are you nervous?' I ask. He's been his usual jovial self all the way over here, but there's something in the way his jaw is set, maybe a stiffness in his demeanour, that's telling me he's as worried as I am about meeting the registrar.

'Nah, we'll be fine,' he says. 'They said this is just so she can meet us before the ceremony. Right?'

'That's what they said. I'm sure this is the normal procedure.' Like I'm an expert on the marriage process. What if it's more than that? When I went back to the registry office to swap Matt for Rafael, they had warned me that they'd have to alert the Home Office in case they had any queries because of Rafael's status. 'You haven't heard anything from the Home Office?' I ask him.

There's the little bulge in his jaw again. 'Nothing yet.'

'Then they're probably not even going to check up on anything. They'd have done it by now, right?'

Rafael doesn't answer my question. Instead, he takes a sheet of paper from his pocket. 'Before we go in,' he says, 'I'd like you to read something. It's from my parents. I translated it for them.'

I take the folded sheet that he hands me.

Dear Nelly,

When Rafael told us he'd met you, our hearts were full of happiness for him, but sadness for ourselves. You may know this one day if you are a parent, but having a child so far away hurts very much. Every day we worry that he is safe and happy and treated well. We wish for him to be close enough to hold in our arms and comfort when he needs it. We want the best for him, always, but that doesn't stop the ache of distance.

So to know that he has met you, his love, and that you will be beside him and wish for him the best, helps ease our pain at missing him so much.

We hope to meet you one day, to hold you in our arms and tell you these things ourselves. Until then, know that we love you because our son does, and wish

you all the happiness on your wedding day and always.
Your future parents-in-law,
David and Patricia Moreno

'Wow, that's so nice,' I say. Somehow my dad's headlock in the kitchen doesn't measure up. 'Are you sad that they won't be there?' Too late, I remember that this is a transaction for him. He wouldn't wish for his parents to be with him to renew his driving license or get his online shopping delivery. This is no different. I only wish it was.

'I would love for them to be here,' he answers, 'but there's no way they can afford it. Plus, they need visas to visit. It's too late now anyway. It's okay. They'll be there on Skype.'

'They're sad, though. I'm sorry about that.'

'Thank you, *mi corazón,*' he says.

I could get lost in the depths of those brown eyes.

We go in to meet with the registrar.

Sally introduces herself as she leads us through the back to one of the town hall's conference rooms. She's very officious-looking with her no nonsense business suit and green glasses hanging from a thin chain around her neck. She takes her time reading through the slim file in front of her. But then she looks up, smiles warmly and I let out the breath I've just realised I'm holding. This will be okay.

She puts her glasses on with a practiced hand. 'Now, this meeting is to verify the information you've declared in relation to your intent to marry, and then to run through what will happen on the day. Okay?'

Verify? Rafael and I reach for each other's hands.

But there's nothing to worry about. Sally goes through the information we've given her: names, parents' names and occupations. 'That was easy,' I say when she's finished.

'I know,' she says. 'It all goes into the public record so we want to be sure it's accurate. Who knows? Someday your great-great-grandchildren might look you up.'

If only that were true.

'So, all that's left is for me to interview each of you,' Sally goes on. 'Would you like to do that together or separately?'

That definitely wasn't in the email she sent me! We're about to be found out. She's going to ask me some tricky question and I won't be able to answer and they'll know this is all a sham. Frantically, as I try to recall every conversation Rafael and I have ever had, I realise how little I know about him. He went to university in Colombia, but he could have gone to public or private school, been head boy or barely scraped by. I have no idea if he's allergic to anything, or broken any bones or whether he's still got his tonsils. I can't even remember if he's left- or right-handed. As for the day-to-day basics like breakfast choice, favourite colour, where he gets his groceries or his brand of toothpaste, how should I know? Thanks to my curry calamity, we've never even brushed our teeth in the same bathroom.

That's because I'm about to marry a virtual stranger. One that I'm madly in love with, but still.

'Together,' we both say.

'All right. Nelly, I'll start with you. What's Rafael's job title?'

'Account Executive for the same company as me. Quality Life Insurance.' That's an easy one to limber me up.

Then Sally looks to Rafael for confirmation. I could have said anything and all he'd have to do is nod! 'Rafael, have you got a business card with you?'

Of course, she's smarter than that. 'And when's Rafael's birthday?'

I'm wracking my brain to remember. 'September eighth. No, seventh. Eighth. Seventh. Seventh.'

'And the year?'

'Nineteen-ninety.' He'll definitely be thirty this year.

'And what will you do to celebrate?'

I can't help but feel that she's going off-piste. 'Erm, we might be on our honeymoon.'

'Where's your honeymoon?'

'I don't know,' I say. 'It's a surprise. Rafael is planning it.'

Rafael does indeed look surprised. But then he says, 'I can't tell you in front of Nelly. Would you like us to . . .?' He gestures towards the door.

'No, no, that's all right. I'm sure it will be lovely. So, Rafael, where was Nelly born?'

'St Ives,' he says. 'Have you been there? There's a gorgeous beach about a mile from her parents' house.'

'Porthminster?' Sally says. 'I have been there. It's a beautiful part of the country.' She closes her notebook. 'Right, that's it, then. The next time I'll see you will be on the big day. Congratulations!'

Rafael grins at me. Then his warm lips meet mine. I lean into him, relieved and happy, even if only for a few more seconds until we go back into the real world.

Chapter 23

Today should be the happiest day of my life (so far). That's what all the magazines say. I'm supposed to be floating on cloud nine, not snivelling into my teacup.

It hit me last night. I mean, it really hit me. I'm marrying the bloke I'm madly in love with. We're about to spend the whole day in a bubble of bliss, appearing to be the most loved-up people on the planet. Except we're really nothing but business partners. The cruelty of that knowledge is shredding me from the inside. Tears pop to my eyes every time I think about it.

'You've got to get hold of yourself,' Rowan says. She turned up at my door before I was even properly awake. She says she was dying to get out of the house, but I know she's here for moral support. 'Nobody is going to believe those are happy tears. You look a wreck. Do you want your mum to see you like this?'

Mum and Dad will be here any minute with Martha and Photo Matt. Not to mention Mabs. Rowan is right. I've got to pull myself together. This is what I wanted.

'Here, blow.' She holds out more tissues. 'I can run out and get you some eye drops if you want.'

'Thanks, could you? I should really shower now.'

I give myself a good talking-to as the hot water runs over me. I'm doing exactly what I set out to do. Look at how well it's already worked. I've got over ten thousand followers now. That's enough to start building up my business. When the final article hits the magazine, my account is going to fly. This is working. I've got to stay focussed on that.

I'll have plenty of time to mend my broken heart after the wedding. Because that will be it, won't it? Rafael and I will go back to our normal lives, apart, as if all this never happened. I'll have my followers and he'll get his visa. Maybe we'll see each other sometimes at one of Jenny's parties or something. I might send him a Christmas card.

My tears mix with the lemony shower gel washing down the plughole.

The doorbell rings as I'm towelling my hair. I forgot to give Rowan a key to let herself back in. 'Sorry, sorry,' I say to the intercom as I hit the door unlock button.

It's a straight shot from the bathroom to the flat's front door. I see it open as I've got my head upside down to apply hair product. 'That was quick,' I say between my legs.

'Are you Nelly?' says a man's voice.

'Oh!' I whip around to find a young bloke holding a bouquet. He looks as mortified as I feel to see me in my not-quite-closing dressing gown.

The blooms he's holding are tied up with twine in pink and orange tissue paper. I peek inside. 'Oh, pretty!'

'Sign here,' he says, handing me his electronic scanner before scarpering out the door.

'Flowers?' says Rowan as she passes the delivery person in the doorway. 'Let's see.'

She peels back the tissue as I search for a clue about who they're from. Although as soon as I see the flowers, I know.

The most breathtakingly romantic heritage pinky-orange roses, big and frilly-edged, are nestled amongst a riot of sherbet-orange lilies and hot pink gerbera. The card reads:

Happy wedding day, mi corazón. You continue to amaze me. Enthral me.
Our future together will be full of laughter, discussion, emotion and love, and I cannot wait to begin it with you.

'From Rafael, I'm guessing, based on your face,' says Rowan.

I swallow my ridiculous grin. He's doing everything a groom could be expected to do. If this was a script, he'd be following it exactly. Then I remember that that's exactly what he's doing. 'It's a nice touch. Mum will like it.'

'Mum will like what?' She and Dad are standing in the doorway.

'How'd you get in?' I ask as they kiss me.

'Someone held the door open downstairs.' Dad is frowning. 'Not very good security.'

'Not when any old riff-raff can wander in.' I hug my dad.

'The flowers,' Rowan tells Mum. 'They're from Rafael.'

'Aren't those nice?' she says. 'I'll find a vase and put on some tea. You get ready. We can't have you being late for your own wedding.'

'Happy wedding day,' says Dad, hugging me again. I bury my face in his shoulder, trying not to drip into his morning coat.

Rowan slips me the eye drops when my parents aren't looking.

Luckily, I'm spared any heartfelt mother-of-the-bride speeches (which would only set me off again) when Martha and Photo Matt turn up with Mabs. A quick check in the mirror next to the intercom confirms that the eye drops are doing their job.

'We are so excited for today!' Martha cries as she hugs me. My glance over her shoulder at Mabs tells me she's not speaking for the whole group. 'We don't want to crash your entire morning, so we'll just get a few pics and then be out of your hair. I was thinking maybe your mum and Mabs helping you into your wedding dress?'

Rowan is staring at Mabs. 'Nice dress,' she says.

'Thank you.' She tugs at the high neckline. That's when I notice her knees.

'Did you shorten that?'

Her face is the picture of innocence. 'I am just tall,' she says.

Uh-huh.

Our car is quiet as I ride with Mum and Dad to the town hall. I can't speak for them, but my tummy is churning faster than my washing machine on the extra-soil setting. I thought I'd obsessed over all the nightmare possibilities since plotting this little caper – getting found out, or going through all the trouble without so much as an extra 'like' to show for it, or being judged for (pretend) falling in love with another man while engaged. But I never imagined that I'd want to chicken out at the last minute.

Now that the time has come, I'm not sure I can stand up in front of everyone I love and tell such a huge lie.

Dad wipes his eyes as they meet mine in the rear-view mirror.

'Are you okay, Dad?'

'Ah, yeah, fine. I'm just remembering when you went to uni,' he says.

'Oh, don't. You'll set me off.'

Everyone had been full of banter until I walked Mum and Dad back to the car when they'd dropped me off. Then Mum said 'love huddle' – our family phrase since I was a child – and all three of us collapsed into a puddle of tears. 'Promise me no love huddles today, okay?' I say. 'My mascara couldn't take it.'

'Sorry, love, I promise. This is a happy day.'

Well, yes. It's supposed to be.

A few of our guests are loitering in front of the town hall when we get there. My eyes scan friends and family, searching for Rafael. He's not there, though. I guess he'll be inside already. I hope so.

Everyone is beaming and snapping photos with their phones while I do my best to return their smiles. 'Wow, you're gorgeous!' Jenny says, carefully kissing my cheek without smudging my make-up.

'Is Rafael here?' I ask.

'Safely inside with Ed. Wait till you see him.'

'I just need a minute,' I tell the guard who shows Mum, Dad and me into a little room off to one side of the entrance. 'Can you please ask them not to start for a few minutes? I just . . .'

The guard holds up his hands. 'Take your time. There's not another ceremony scheduled until three.' His manner is so kind that I could kiss him. Instead, I feel tears threaten to water down my make-up.

When he closes the door, Mum takes my hand. 'It's perfectly normal to be nervous,' she says. 'I was, wasn't I?'

Dad laughs. 'I wasn't sure her dad was going to get her down the aisle. It's all right, love. It's normal.'

I can't tell them how not normal this is. I can't tell anyone. I might be getting married in a few minutes, but I've never felt so alone in my life.

Taking a deep breath, we start for the council chamber room where Rafael is waiting.

Mum is on one side, Dad on the other, with Mabs behind me (no doubt glowering) as my entrance song starts. If they didn't have their arms linked through mine, I'm not sure I'd be standing. I just want this to be over.

The guard opens the double doors to the large room, and we walk through. My lips are wobbling as I try to smile. Seeing everyone so happy does help. I can do this.

Then I see Rafael, smiling at the front, and my wobbly smile steadies. His suit is a gorgeous shade of blue. There's not a purple check in sight.

There is a pink and green jungle motif bow tie, though.

'Wow,' he says when I reach him at the front. I can tell he's as surprised by my dress as I am by his suit. 'Nice legs.'

I glance down at my shoes, then my knees. I will never admit that Mabs was right, but the second the tailor showed me her minidress handiwork, I fell in love with it. With its three-quarter-length pearl-encrusted lace sleeves, high neckline and the sheerest pale pink tights I've ever imagined, it's got such a sixties mod vibe about it.

'Nice bow tie,' I tell him.

He touches it. 'It's growing on me.'

'It does look like it's growing. You've worn that for me? You didn't have to.'

'I know. I wanted to.'

Formally, he shakes my dad's hand and kisses Mum on the cheek. 'Thank you for having your daughter,' he tells them. Then he embraces Mabs. *'Te amo,'* I hear her whisper to him before she goes to sit with the other guests, where she'll stay until we need her to sign the marriage certificate.

The registrar, Sally, starts officiously, but I barely hear her words. This all feels so real that I can hardly believe it's not. How I want to stay tucked up cosy in this world, where today, this moment, is the start of the happiest time in my life and I'm about to share my true feelings with the man I love.

'This place in which we are now met,' Sally intones, 'has been duly sanctioned, according to law, for the celebration of marriages. You are here today to witness the joining in matrimony of Helen Elizabeth Fraser and Rafael David Moreno Cortes. If any person present knows of any lawful impediment to this marriage, he or she should declare it now.'

I'm aware of a rising tide of murmurs coming from behind us. Rafael's face drops as he scans the guests. I turn around.

Matt is sitting beside Mabs. With his hand up.

'What are you doing here?' I hiss, as if the entire room can't hear me.

'He is my date,' says Mabs, calm as you please.

'That's sick. Both of you. Perverse, but whatever.' I glance over at Photo Matt, but his camera is lowered. Some things are too unbelievable even for a gossip magazine.

'I'd like to say something,' Matt says. 'Nelly can't marry this bloke because she and I love each other.'

'No, we don't, Matt. Now, please sit down.' Or, better yet, leave.

Sally is looking at me for some guidance. Like I've got any.

It's Rafael who breaks the awkward silence. 'Could Nelly and I have a moment?'

'Sure, of course,' Sally says. 'There's a room just through that door.' She points behind her. 'Take your time. We'll be here.'

Rafael takes my hand and leads me through the door. My heart is pounding.

'*Mi corazón*,' he says once we're alone. 'Do you want to do this?'

His eyes are so kind that the tears spill over in mine. I'm not sure that even my waterproof mascara is up for this job. 'I don't know,' I whisper. 'It seemed like such a good idea back when we said we would. Didn't it? Good for both of us. But now I don't know.'

Gently, so gently, he wipes my cheek. 'I understand. This hasn't been as easy as I thought.'

Of course it hasn't. Between my constant photo-taking and worrying about how many likes I'm getting and trying to shove him into my idea of the perfect wedding just because it's what I imagined I wanted, I was probably a nightmare. What about him? This is about him too. I wish I'd realised that sooner. 'I'm so sorry.'

'You should be with a man who can love you the way you deserve.'

'I'm sorry,' I say again, because I feel like such a fool. I might be in love, but Rafael clearly isn't. That's what he's telling me. I need to listen now.

'I will stand aside,' he says. 'The visa doesn't matter.'

'Of course it does. Rafael, you'll have to leave if we don't do this.'

He shrugs. 'You are more important than that. If Matt will make you happy, then this is wrong. You should be with him.'

I'm pretty sure I do one of those comedy double-takes. 'What?! I don't want to marry Matt!'

Now he looks confused. 'Who, then?'

You know what? I'm so bloody tired of spending every waking minute worrying about how I come across to everyone else. Frankly, I don't care if nobody 'likes' me ever again.

'You, Rafael. You're who I want to marry. But it doesn't matter because I'll get over it eventually, so let's just get this done, then you can have your visa.'

'Ah, *mi corazón*, why must you make things difficult?'

'Me? Matt's the one who just pulled off the scene from *The Graduate*.' He's shaking his head. 'Where Dustin Hoffman bangs on the glass in the church? It's a classic . . . Doesn't matter.'

'No, *mi corazón*, it doesn't matter. What matters is your feelings.'

'I know, like I said, I'm sorry, I'll get over them. I promise not to turn into some kind of stalker person just because we've got a piece of paper that says we're married. You won't regret getting your visa this way.'

'The visa doesn't matter,' he says again. 'I will probably need to leave anyway.'

'What are you talking about?'

'The Home Office are investigating. I received a notice. So, you see, *mi corazón*, no matter how much I want to stay here, no matter that my heart is here.' He reaches towards my face but stops himself. 'I can't do what I'd love to do.'

'What would you love to do?' I'm whispering now.

'This.' When his warm lips meet mine, my legs nearly give way with relief. 'For the rest of my life,' he says, 'this.'

'Oh, but you can,' I murmur. Then I kiss him back.

'It isn't fair to our hearts, because we might not be able to stay together.'

I pull back from him. 'When did you hear from the Home Office?'

'That night we had dinner in Soho.'

'But you've carried on with all this . . . for me?'

'Yes, of course. I would do anything for you.'

'Is that true, Rafael?'

'Of course it is. If you'd said you still had feelings for Matt, then I would have told you to be with him, because I love you, *mi corazón*. *Estoy enamorado de ti,* as much as I didn't want to.'

'Thanks.'

He laughs. 'Only because I might have to leave you and that would break my heart. But please know that I would do anything to make you happy.'

His expression could not be more sincere. Finally, this is real.

'Then I want you to do something now,' I say. 'I want you to go back out there and marry me, because, Rafael, I love you more than I ever thought it was possible to love anyone. I don't care what happens with the Home Office. Whatever it is, we'll deal with it together.'

'In a minute,' he says. 'Let this moment be only for us.' His lips meet mine again.

Then we go back to our wedding.

Everyone in the world that we love is clapping and cheering as Sally says, 'Ladies and gentlemen, it gives me great pleasure to introduce Nelly and Rafael, the newlyweds!' Gran is whooping beside my brother and Rowan. No doubt Caitlin and Leo are encouraging her. My girlfriends are hugging my mum, and Dad keeps wiping his eyes while Ed scoots behind us to kiss Jenny. Weddings really do bring out the best in people. Even Rafael's parents are here, via Skype, anyway, smiling at us from Rafael's laptop screen.

He sweeps me up into his arms again. 'You've already kissed the bride,' I say.

'I never want to stop kissing her.'

'That's authentic.'

'It truly is.'

Chapter 24

Another cheer goes up as Rafael and I get to the reception, although we have to go out to the deck to find our guests. I don't blame them. It's a beautiful warm day and the sun is sparkling on the reservoir and reflecting off the caps of the swimmers racing further along the shore. Far from being distracting, hearing the starting horns and shouts from the coaches adds to the atmosphere. Rafael was right. It would be perfect for swimming. I glance at my dress. Maybe not in this, though.

Someone hands me a glass of champagne while everyone mobs us for kisses and congratulations. 'You look really, actually happy,' Rowan mutters into my ear. 'If I didn't know better . . .'

'He loves me!' I whisper back.

On that news, Rowan throws her arms around Rafael. 'Welcome to the family,' she tells him. Photo Matt has his camera aimed at us. I wonder if anyone will be able to tell the difference from the photos. I feel like I'm glowing now. Maybe Matt will snap a happy aura around me or something.

Inside, the room looks exactly as perfect as I imagined it would. Well, not as I *originally* imagined . . .

The sun glinting through the huge windows makes hundreds of colourful paper lanterns glow. With the front and back doors flung open, they sway gently in the breeze. The gorgeously vintage-looking white linen tablecloths set off the roses and wild array of tropical flowers that tumble from all the jam jars. Later, when the sun goes down, the hurricane candles will twinkle amongst them. By then our guests should have found all the gaily-wrapped Colombian and old-fashioned English retro sweets tucked in amongst the table arrangements. Hopefully it won't ruin everyone's appetites, because they're going to love the salmon dinner.

The band is already set up in one corner, though it's Frank Sinatra crooning from the speakers at the moment. Later it will be merengue. Rafael is right. Everyone will love having the falafel truck parked up out front when they get peckish after all the dancing.

'Stand just there,' Photo Matt says to us. 'Great background.'

Rafael plucks a strawberry-iced donut from one of the pegs. 'Mmm, want a bite?' I admit that an entire wall of donuts does make a great photo opp. They're all glazed – pink, yellow, orange and lilac – with contrasting drizzle. Not that I'm taking any pics myself today. I'm off-duty.

'You're supposed to wait till after . . . Yes, please.' I take a bite, then kiss Rafael's sticky lips. 'We get to do whatever we want now.'

'Together,' he says.

'With no cameras.'

'One more camera.' He nods towards the photo booth. I lead him there by the hand.

Choosing the bushiest moustache in the dressing-up box and a cowboy hat, I settle myself beside Rafael as he holds false eyelashes to his face. 'One, two, three, smile!'

I've got one eye closed.

It's perfect.

'Mabs, come take a picture with us,' Rafael says when he sees her hovering near the booth. She's dateless. Matt didn't follow her here. I caught sight of him after the ceremony as he turned to walk away from us. Even though I know he never wanted to marry me, I do feel sorry for him. I hope he finds the person he can't wait to spend the rest of his life with. Nobody deserves anything less.

If there's one downside to all this, it's that from today onwards, Mabs will be in my life. I guess I'd better try to get used to that. Rafael loves her, so maybe she isn't all bad.

'That suits you,' she says of my impressive 'tache.

I move it to my bikini line. 'Is it noticeable? Do you think I should get it lasered?'

Her giggle sounds real. I still won't apologise for her dress, though. Not just yet.

A chant starts up out on the deck. 'What's that?'

It's my father. He's pouring shots for everyone from a bottle of tequila. 'No, Dad,' I say. 'No. Rafael, seriously, you know what will happen.' Where's Mum? She can usually talk sense into him.

Dad tries to hand me a shot glass. 'Lighten up, Nelly, it's your wedding day.'

His words are exactly the reminder I need. What am I so afraid of anyway? That everyone will have too much fun? I take a glass. 'Here's to a wonderful life,' I say.

'A wonderful life!'

The shots go down. Blurgh. I hate tequila.

'It does look nice and cool,' I tell Rafael as we look out over the water. 'Almost nice enough for a swim.'

'You're joking,' he says. 'What about your hair?'

'What about it?' Even before I was engaged to Matt, I knew what my wedding hair would look like: a glossy chignon scattered with seed pearls.

'Won't you want photos for later?' Rafael asks.

'Let them snap me happy and in love.'

'And naked?' he adds. 'I don't have my swimsuit on under here, do you?'

That should be the end of my whimsy. Who jumps into a lake on their wedding day anyway? It's not sensible. It'll probably ruin the rest of the photos for the final feature.

'Mabs?' I call to her. 'Can you go to the shop for us, please? It's just next to reception at the water sports centre.'

I'm sure I see a smile playing around her lips. I like to think it's because she sees that Rafael and I are truly happy together.

She doesn't take long to return with her purchases. She

holds up my swimsuit without a whisper of a smile. It's about as flattering as a horse blanket, with its ridiculously low-cut granny pant leg line that still manages to squeeze some of my bum out the back. No, I won't be apologising for her dress today.

'Do you want to tell anyone what we're doing?' Rafael asks when we're standing, barefoot, in the empty corridor outside the changing rooms. 'Martha, or maybe Matt for a photo?'

'No, it doesn't matter. Let's just be us.'

I can go back to being an *influencer* after our honeymoon. Until then, I'm just plain old Nelly on cloud nine.

We walk out onto the deck in our suits. Laughter rises up from everyone.

'Ready?' I say. 'One, two, three!'

We hold hands and jump together.

#authentic.

THE END